PRAISE FOR MICHAEL GRANT JAFFE'S
DANCE REAL SLOW

"A sensitive, well-observed and loving book. . . . Jaffe sees the beauty, the sweet silliness, the frustration, the fragile joy of parenthood and understands the way it is a blinding passion for those not merely called but chosen."
—*Los Angeles Times Book Review*

"*Dance Real Slow* marks the debut of a very gifted young writer."
—Lorrie Moore

"[A] delicate and complex portrait of fatherhood, one that is refreshingly persuasive."
—*Time Out New York*

"A full-hearted novel about a man's love for his child. . . . A winner!"
—Los Angeles Features Syndicate

"Enormously likable . . . right on the mark."
—Larry Watson

"As he enumerates the rituals of his life with Calvin . . . the exhausting cycle of care to which every single parent is bound becomes comically, painfully vivid. Yet Jaffe describes these everyday rhythms with such metaphorical grace and precision that his prose seems a manifestation of Nash's love for his son."
—*The New Yorker*

"Wonderful. . . . [Jaffe] dares to allow the tenderness and satisfaction of loving a child to rival the passion of loving a woman."
—Rosellen Brown

"A tender and believable portrayal of a father's emotional fabric . . . remarkable . . . satisfying."
—*San Antonio Express-News*

"Absorbing, introspective. . . . Captures the small, intimate, humorous details of a child's life as well as the fierce, protective love of a single father tormented by doubts and fears. Recommended."
—*Library Journal*

"Powerful. . . . A stirring and worthwhile read."
—*Swing*

"A first novel of considerable warmth and strength."
—*The Star-Ledger*, Newark, NJ

DANCE REAL SLOW

MICHAEL GRANT JAFFE

DANCE REAL SLOW

BANTAM BOOKS

New York Toronto London Sydney Auckland

This edition contains the complete text of the original hardcover edition.
NOT ONE WORD HAS BEEN OMITTED.

DANCE REAL SLOW

A Bantam Book / published by arrangement with Farrar, Straus and Giroux

PUBLISHING HISTORY
Farrar, Straus and Giroux edition published 1996
Bantam edition / July 1997

Grateful acknowledgment is made for permission to reprint excerpts from Rock Springs *by Richard Ford, with permission of Grove/Atlantic, Inc. Copyright © 1987. "Lonely Ol' Night," words and music by John Mellencamp, with permission of Warner Brothers. Copyright © 1985 Windswept Pacific Entertainment Co. d/b/a Full Keel Music Co. "You Can Close Your Eyes," words and music by James Taylor, with permission of EMI Blackwood Music Inc. Copyright © 1971 EMI Blackwood Music Inc. and Country Road Music Inc.*

Library of Congress Catalog Card Number: 95-30645.

For information address: Farrar, Straus and Giroux, 19 Union Square West, New York, New York 10003.

ISBN 0-553-57709-3

Published simultaneously in the United States and Canada

Bantam Books are published by Bantam Books, a division of Bantam Doubleday Dell Publishing Group, Inc. Its trademark, consisting of the words "Bantam Books" and the portrayal of a rooster, is Registered in U.S. Patent and Trademark Office and in other countries. Marca Registrada. Bantam Books, 1540 Broadway, New York, New York 10036.

PRINTED IN THE UNITED STATES OF AMERICA

RAD 10 9 8 7 6 5 4 3 2 1

For my mother

and the rest of my family

Special thanks to John Glusman and Farrar, Straus and Giroux, Peter Scott, and Cindy Klein, the best friend and literary agent any writer could ever want.

Also, I wish to thank Morin Bishop, David Bauer, Steve Rushin and all my friends at Sports Illustrated, *Bertis Downs and Mike Mills and the rest of the world's best band, Georges and Anne Borchardt, the Hamilton and Henkel families, Lynn Cox, and Lorrie Moore.*

The answer is simple: it is just low-life, some coldness in us all, some helplessness that causes us to misunderstand life when it is pure and plain, makes our existence seem like a border between two nothings, and makes us no more or less than animals who meet on the road—watchful, unforgiving, without patience or desire.

—RICHARD FORD, *Great Falls*

ONE

Calvin eats dirt. He never actually swallows it, just places loose clumps onto his tongue and sucks, I think. It reminds him of the powder I sprinkle into his milk—dark, chocolaty. Often, I grab the back of his head, forcing him to spit it out, squeezing his tongue like an anchovy and stroking it with the corner of my shirt. Mostly, I worry he may choke on a stone or stick, like this afternoon, when I found him coughing, hacking up muddy phlegm that clung like a web to his lower lip. I reached into his mouth, hard, pulling out a twig pressed against his uvula. He knows better, my son, but he is still young and needs to be watched.

The sky quiets with deep orange and loose, heavy smudges of purple. A small patch of well-trodden dirt rests at the bottom of a low, sloping incline, carved from a field thick with tall, slender sheaths of wheat. Standing alone, just above this push of gold, sits a twisted piece of maple, one foot wide and ten feet high. A weathered plank is nailed in at its top, the flat side perpendicular to the ground, with a rusted basketball rim jutting out an inch or so below-center. The rim is slightly bent and uneven in places. Soiled fragments of net hang still, like grapes.

Poised beyond, where the grass starts tanned and stiff, I lie cross-legged, holding a long-necked bottle of beer pressed between my thumb and lower forefinger. I take a sip. The beer is warm and I let it stay in my mouth for a while before swallowing. Calvin looks briefly in my direction before hoisting another shot toward the battered backboard. The ball is much too large for him and after he releases it the momentum causes him to fall backwards, on his ass. The ball makes a tiny parabola, arcing well short of its target and thumping into the dirt. Calvin has been at this for almost ten minutes and I can see that he is getting tired. Again, he lifts himself, dragging the toes of his sneakers as he moves to retrieve the ball. He leans over, placing his cheek against its worn leather surface. A miniature ostrich.

"You want some dessert?" I yell.

He does not answer. He just stays there with his little Jockey short waistband hiked several inches above his blue jeans. I take another drink of beer and adjust myself, lifting the right side of my rear and resettling it on the ground. Finally, he takes one hand off the ball and reaches for something in the shadows. He turns so that his back is now completely toward me and then stands, lifting both hands to his chest. After a moment he pivots and faces me.

"I'll eat some ice cream," he says, matter-of-factly.

"I'm sure you will."

He begins walking in my direction, pressing his right hand gently against the pocket of his T-shirt.

"Where are you going?" I ask.

He stops and rubs his chin with the heel of his hand. He scrunches in his forehead, tight.

"What'd you forget?"

Calvin heads back to get the ball. He holds it out front, against his stomach, like a pregnant woman's belly.

"Got it?" I ask, pouring the last finger or so of beer into the prickly peppergrass.

He nods and the two of us walk up to the house. Midway, Calvin stops and places the ball down at his feet. He lets out a slight breath and then picks the ball up and begins walking again. When we reach the porch he drops it into a large wicker basket beside the door, right on top of a small orange football, a plastic lemon attached to a black cord that wraps around your ankle so that you can swing the lemon with one leg and skip over it with the other, and a twisted pair of convenience-store sunglasses.

In the light of the kitchen I can see Calvin is filthy. He has bruises of dirt above both cheeks and a broad band of dust horseshoed about the front of his neck.

"We're gonna clean up a bit before ice cream," I say, placing my hand over his shoulder blades and guiding him to the stairs. In the bathroom he pulls out a small stepladder below the sink and climbs up, removing a washcloth from the rail.

"I think we're gonna need a shower here, pal," I tell him.

He is not listening. He is on his toes, stretching to reach the faucet knobs, his pelvis pressed against the base of the sink. I grab him from behind, sliding my hands into his armpits and lowering him to the floor.

"Straight up," I say, grabbing the sleeves of his shirt. He cocks his head and looks away, at the window behind me. Slowly his arms become rigid above his head, hands opening like sunflowers.

"What's this?" I ask, feeling a wet spot. I spread his shirt over the countertop, lightly touching a smear of dampness below the pocket. I reach in and remove a small brown slug.

"Jesus. What are you doing with this, Cal?"

He is now staring down at his bare stomach. It is taut and tanned and he is pulling at a fold of skin above his belly button.

"Where did you get this?"

"Playing basketball," he says, his chin still on his chest.

"Well, don't pick these up anymore. They're dirty and icky and I don't want you handling them. Understand?"

He gives a little nod.

"What'd you want with this, anyway?" I ask, wrapping the slug in a ribbon of toilet paper and flushing it.

"I don't know. I just wanted it," he says, his voice trailing off near the end.

"Slugs are the same as worms, Cal. Remember what I told you about worms? Worms are not pets. Neither are slugs. People don't get up in the morning to take their slugs for a walk. They're nasty."

I slip my hand into the front of his jeans and yank him over, unfastening the top button.

"Up," I say, tapping the edge of the tub. He sits, holding my shoulder for support, while I pull off his pants and underwear. I undress quickly, leaving my own clothing in a pile beside Calvin's. The two of us step into the tub, Calvin grabbing the back of my knees. Pointing the nozzle down, I turn on the shower, adjusting the water temperature before I lead him around front. He hands me the soap and I wash his face, his back. I pour a dollop of shampoo into my hand and then wipe some of it into his hair and the rest into mine.

"Okay, eggbeater," I say, lathering my scalp. Calvin does the same, squeezing his eyes closed as pencil-thin streaks of shampoo channel down the front of his face. After a few minutes I wrap my arm around his hips and lift him, tilting the back of his head into the widening spray of the shower nozzle. His hands are cupped over his eyes. I bury my fingers in his hair, fanning out the remainder of shampoo; I shift my elbow over his waist, away from his sardine-sized penis flicking beneath the water's thin shimmer.

"That's it," I say, pulling back a corner of the curtain. "Use your blue towel, the one next to the hamper."

I rinse off and then step out, gathering my hair into a stubby clump at the base of my neck and squeezing the excess water down my back. Calvin has left moist footprints, the size of a large dog's paws, on the bathroom mat.

"Calvin, come back here."

He returns to the doorway, naked and dripping.

"Did you dry yourself?"

He shrugs.

"Come here."

I remove the towel from around my waist and give him a once-over, rubbing his face as I might a shoe. He moans, but only for a moment.

"Okay, now I want to put some powder on you," I say, sprinkling the powder onto my palms and touching him where he chaffs: underneath his arms, between his thighs.

"Pajamas," I yell to him as he starts down the hallway. "And bring your towel back in here."

Calvin sits on the counter beside the stove, his feet dangling, tapping against the cupboard door beneath. He is holding two teaspoons like drumsticks across his lap. He watches me pry out large wedges of ice cream and knock them into our dishes.

"I want sauce," he says, banging the spoons together.

"We don't have any. We'll get some more the next time we go shopping."

"Let's go now."

"We're not going now," I say, running hot water over the serving spoon. "It's too late. The store is closed."

"Why?"

"What'd you mean, why? Because the people who run stores have to go home to their families, too. Shouldn't they get to have dinner?"

Calvin is still for a minute, digging the edge of a spoon into the spongy roll of skin behind his chin.

"They can eat," he says. "Just not when we want sauce."

I smile. "I'll let them know that."

"Let them know," he starts, climbing down. "For next time."

The two of us sit at the table and eat our bowls of French vanilla ice cream. Calvin uses his spoon like a spade, grabbing it down low near where the handle vanishes into the flat well of metal. The ice cream is turning soft and it has begun to slither its way around Calvin's wrist and up his arm.

"Maybe we should have showered afterwards," I tell him, reaching over to wipe the hollow, open side of his elbow.

His hair is almost dry, spiky and tight above the rise of his forehead, stiff as straw. It is yellow, with clefts of brown buried deep and random.

"Done?" I ask, taking both bowls to the sink.

"Well," he says, his chest wavering with quick, short breaths. "Well, do we have more? 'Cuz I could eat more."

"No more tonight. You've had plenty."

"Yeah, but . . . but." He moves over to my side, his hands sticky and anxious, twisting above his waist. "If I . . . maybe . . . I'll just have a little."

"You won't have a little. It's getting late and—here"—I hand him a damp towel—"wipe up. You've got ice cream all over yourself."

I am reminded of a time before Kate left, when she was still pregnant and we were visiting my parents in Ohio. It was late November, before Thanksgiving, and the air had just turned cold. Kate and I had decided to take a drive in the country, away from Lakeshire, away from Cleveland. After a while we pulled off to the side of a small gravel road, beside a narrow bend in the Chagrin River, and sat in the car watching the water run from black to foamy white and then back to black again. I stroked her arms, which were draped steady over her bloated belly. We didn't talk for a long time, resting still, listening to the rush of water through her open window. Finally, Kate turned to me and said in a low, throaty whisper that she needed something. I leaned over, moving my hand to the softness below her breasts, and kissed her on the neck and then full on the lips. We kissed deep and wet for a few more minutes, my hand moving down, brushing over the embryonic Calvin on its way to Kate's inner thighs. Then she started to laugh, saying this isn't what she had in mind when she said she needed something. What she had wanted was something sweet, like pudding or ice cream.

There was a small New England-style town called Gates Mills about a half mile from where the car was parked, and Kate waited while I went off to surprise her. The houses were clean and white, with slate roofs and a common white fence that held off the road. I attended high school not far from there, and in the spring, before baseball practice, we would drive to Henry's, a general store, where we would buy bubble gum, chewing tobacco, sunflower seeds, and sodas. I hated the chewing tobacco, so I bought licorice, which turned my spit brown without making me ill.

Henry's was still there, unchanged, and I left it

much as I had in high school, with a paper bag of two-cent candy: mostly caramels, peppermints, red-hots, and jawbreakers; and a pint of mocha chip ice cream, which was Kate's favorite. On my way back to the car it began snowing heavy flakes, big as feathers. Kate was standing down by the river, breath pushing in bursts from her face. I came up behind, taking her gently by the elbow and then the forearm. She told me my teeth and lips were red. I opened the bag and pointed inside and she nodded as we walked back to the car. I had forgotten to get spoons, so we carved out chunks of ice cream using keys. And when we were finished we went back to the river and washed off, using a T-shirt I had in the trunk to dry ourselves. At one point, while Kate was bending low to cup the cold water to her mouth, snow settling evenly on her hair and shoulders, I remember thinking I loved her more than anyone else, more than I could possibly love anyone else. That I would never stop loving her. But, of course, I was wrong. I could love someone more. And, indeed, we could stop loving each other. For as powerful and encompassing as love is, during brief moments, it turns fragile, needing desperately to be protected.

Calvin and I finish in the kitchen and I take him upstairs to bed. From the time he was a baby, he has always been easy to put to sleep; it has never been a struggle.

Calvin's room is across the hall from mine, next to the bathroom. It is bright and spare and I have promised to paint large dinosaurs on the walls in green and purple when I have the time. He also wants a big blue barn beside the doorway, below the end of his bed. I have told him that most barns are red, or at the least brown, but he seems unfazed, stoic. He wants his blue.

I close the window while he brushes his teeth. He is good about this, too, never needing to be told. He slides into bed and I pull the covers up close to his face. Leaning over, I kiss him lightly on the cheek and nose and whisper I love him.

The air is thin and active, pushing V-shaped parts into the front of my hair. I stand on the porch smoking a cigarette, breaking the ashes off against the wooden railing. The final draft of Roby Edwards's last will and testament sits flapping on the end of an aluminum-and-vinyl lawnchair. I did not go to law school to ensure that the estate of the third largest landowner in eastern Kansas was equitably divided among his family; things have simply worked out that way.

At 41,094, Tarent, Kansas, is the seventh largest city in the state—just ahead of Hutchinson and behind Salina. Tarent is twenty-two miles west of Lawrence, where the University of Kansas is located, and about sixty miles east of Kansas State, which is in Manhattan. The route to either is easy. Manhattan is 70 West into Topeka, then switch over to 50. Lawrence is 50 East all the way. I drive to one of the schools weekly to use the law library. Tarent's public library is small, and most of its legal section concerns itself only with basics. Exactly three and one quarter shelves of it, beginning with William B. Anderson's 1964 manual entitled *Constitutional*

Law and ending with Jerome Wiley's twice checked out *Defense for Hard-Core Offenders*. There are also quite a few legal volumes at the firm I work for, Blyth & Blyth, although we, too, are small. Just three lawyers, including myself.

I met Harper Blyth at Michigan, during my second week of law school. He lived down the hall from me in one of the few single rooms in our dormitory. I remember first encountering him after returning from a student-union showing of *It's a Wonderful Life* with Jimmy Stewart, which seemed to be a strange film for the university to play in late September. My roommate was Michael Bennett and the two of us were walking up the stairway to our floor. Michael was telling me how during Christmas his sophomore year of high school he had mononucleosis and was bedridden for nearly five weeks. He said the local television stations in Richmond, Virginia, where he was from, had shown *It's a Wonderful Life* nine times during that period and he had watched every airing. All except the last twenty minutes of the seventh broadcast, when he passed out from the codeine pills they had given him for his swollen throat. His girlfriend at the time had brought over a giant stuffed frog and placed it above the television set. The frog had a sign around his neck that read "Get Better Quick," but his younger brother had crossed out the word "Quick" and had written next to it in red marker "Dick." So now every time Michael sees *It's a Wonderful Life* he can't help but think of the obscene frog once perched on his television.

Michael had just finished telling this story and the

two of us were on our floor, standing next to a soda machine, when we heard a low-pitched crack, like the sound of an ax striking wood, followed by the breaking of glass. We heard someone yell out he was sorry, that it was *his* mistake. Michael and I moved around the corner, looking down the long hallway. Near one end, alone, Harper Blyth was sweeping shards of glass from a fire-extinguisher cabinet into a pile against the wall. He was using a polo mallet like a push broom. He was dressed in complete polo attire: a white helmet and jodhpurs, a navy shirt with a thick horizontal bar of white across his chest, and large brown riding boots.

"What the hell are you doing?" asked Michael.

"Oh. Well—" Harper looked around for something to whisk the glass onto, like a newspaper. "See, it's my birthday and—you wouldn't know where I could get a dustpan?"

"You're dressed like that because it's your birthday?" said Michael.

I handed Harper a magazine someone had abandoned on a chair.

"Thanks," he said, opening the magazine to the middle, where the staples rise like Braille. "No—or *yes*, I guess I am dressed like this because it's my birthday. Actually, my father sent the stuff."

"A present?"

"Yeah."

"Do you play?" asked Michael.

"Nope," Harper said, balancing the broken glass, piled in sparkling heaps, over to a trash barrel. "In fact,

I don't think I've ever even been on a horse. Except maybe when I was little, at one of those riding zoos or someplace."

At that point, I did not think I would ever have much to do with Harper Blyth. Not for any particular reason, other than I didn't think he was the kind of person with whom an aspiring attorney should associate.

When I wake up, Calvin is standing at the foot of my bed, wet again. The rain is steady, like an engine, and Calvin has gone outside in only his pajama bottoms and a large sombrero that my mother brought back from Mexico.

"You're not normal," I tell him, into my pillow.

"Are you gettin' up?"

He moves around to the side of the bed, near where my face is mashed against the stiff ridge of the mattress.

"Why did you go outside?" I ask him softly.

"To get Moonie," he says, lowering his head to see if my eyes are open. Moonie is our neighbor Mrs. Grafton's cat. I lie still, breathing easy for several minutes. Finally, I roll from my side onto my back, staring straight up at the stucco ceiling.

"Calvin, where is Moonie?"

Calvin reaches over, grabbing the blanket above my chest and hoisting himself on the bed. He lifts up his leg, straddling my stomach, his knees pressed firmly against my rib cage.

"Oh, she's okay."

"Where's okay?"

"She's drying off," Calvin says, shoving his wet face onto my shoulder, the sombrero slipping down the side of his back. "In the basement. With the clothes."

"Good," I say. "With the clothes."

I remain motionless for a few moments longer and then, as if on command, sit up, erect, knocking Calvin backwards onto my shins. I hurl from bed and run down both flights of stairs, until I reach our laundry room. The dryer is off, but I open the door anyway, peering inside. Calvin is behind me.

"Sheesh, Dad," he says, his hands cupped together above his groin.

My chest slows as I stand. Looking across the room, I can see the clothesline is moving, rocking uneasily with the awkward rhythms of an EKG. There is a gray laundry bag hanging from the line, six clothespins fastening it along the top. Moonie is struggling to escape, her tiny claws tearing at the nylon. A stool sits off to the side with a puddle, smooth as linoleum, centered at its base. I undo the bag, and as I pull apart the drawstrings, Moonie scurries across the hard cement floor, trying to find a place to hide. A place to hide from my son.

"See, Calvin," I say, taking him by the elbow and leading him toward Moonie. "Now she's scared of you."

"She ain't a-scared. She just wants to play or something."

The two of us walk out of the laundry area, into an adjoining room that is dark and mostly empty except for six or seven large boxes stacked in a far corner. Calvin runs ahead, and when he reaches the boxes, he falls to his knees and starts crawling on all fours. He is making a squeaking sound, calling out for Moonie. The cat wants nothing to do with Calvin and she digs into one of the rear boxes and begins scaling it until she slips over the edge and inside. I reach down, placing my hand below the cat's front legs, pulling her free. Her claws are caught on a sweater and she brings it halfway out before it drops loose. Calvin comes over to me, taking the cat into his arms, against his chest.

"See, she's *not* scared."

The cat looks terrified and she struggles to climb away from Calvin—across his shoulder and down his back. But Calvin is quick and he adjusts Moonie along his sternum.

"Does Mrs. Grafton know you have Moonie?" I ask, picking up the sweater.

"I s'pose," Calvin says.

"Suppose nothing. You take her back over there."

I lift the wool sweater to my face, inhaling deeply when it reaches my nose. Beneath the pungent ammonia stench of mothballs, it smells faintly of Kate.

"Here," I say to Calvin. "Slip this on."

"That's not mine."

"I know," I answer, holding Moonie in one hand while I pull the sweater down over Calvin's head. I roll the sleeves up several times. "It's your mother's."

He is unimpressed. He takes back the cat and walks toward the staircase, the hem of the sweater flapping a few inches above his feet.

"And before you go over there, put on your boots."

He lets out a small huff and then climbs away.

This morning her hair is pulled back tight, into a small blond plume at the back of her head, fastened with a floppy, oversized ribbon. She is wearing a white blouse beneath a pair of coarse, new overalls. Calvin waves to her from the passenger seat of the car.

"Listen, I'm coming by early today—remind Charlotte," I say to him, combing the hair out of his face with my fingertips. "I told her last night, just remind her."

Meg is still standing in the doorway, adjusting one of the overall straps against her shoulder. She is Calvin's closest friend. Her mother, Charlotte, watches the two of them most days, while I am at work. Kneeling up, Calvin kisses my cheek and then slams the door behind him. Both Meg and I watch as he navigates the soggy pathway to the house. Part of me imagines that Meg wants to see Calvin slip, landing face-first in a kidney-shaped puddle of creamy mud. She has a dark side not normally so well defined in a child her age. Once, I saw her squish a ladybug beneath her thumb and then smear it down her nose, like war paint. Another time, she took a barbed pine branch and wrapped it around her neck, a fallen crown, yanking until it turned her throat red with irritation. Charlotte hopes she will outgrow this behavior and, truthfully, so do I.

When Calvin reaches the porch, he turns and gives me a forward nod, as he does most mornings, as if to say, "Go *on*, already."

The car's stick shift sometimes has trouble with reverse, like today. You have to move it into neutral and shake it with quick, short snaps of your wrists, as if making popcorn in a pot. The car is a cream-colored 1966 Volvo station wagon that belonged to my maternal grandfather, Sanford Blaine. He gave it to me for my seventeenth birthday, four months before he moved from Akron to Phoenix. My father did not want me to have it; he didn't think I needed a car and he certainly didn't think I was responsible enough to own one. So, the day after my grandfather brought it over, my father took a baseball bat and caved in both the front and rear windshields. He told me when I could afford to have them replaced I could drive the car. He also told me to sweep up the glass. It took me nine weeks, working two jobs—one before school and one after—before I got new windshields. Three days after I was driving again, the carburetor went. That took me another five weeks to replace.

I pull onto Kenimore, which is a long two-lane stretch of road that fills most of Tarent. It will take me to Mercer Street, at the center of town, a block from my office. My father was like that, with the windshield and all. He was used to getting his way and making a point in doing so.

When I was nine months old he quite suddenly moved the family from Des Moines, Iowa, to Lakeshire, Ohio, outside Cleveland, and in the twenty-six years that followed he served as the men's head basketball coach at Eastern Ohio University. He took the Eagles to fourteen straight NCAA basketball tournaments, eighteen overall. He also won a national championship, in 1979, and was runner-up two other times. I have his national championship ring in a blue velvet box at the back of my underwear drawer, along with a St. Michael's medallion that was given to him when he was born, and a knuckle of mashed gold—unrecognizable as his wedding band. It had once gotten caught in a lawnmower, along with his finger, and he never bothered to have it restored.

World's Loudest Frog reads the cardboard sign, written in dark green marker and stapled to the side of a small wooden crate resting near the walkway to my office. A thin-limbed boy is kneeling in lemon grass, stroking the aforementioned frog with his bony fingers.

"He's not feeling so good," says the boy as I pause before passing.

"I'm sorry to hear that."

"Gave him too many crickets. He likes water bugs better."

"He's loud, though, huh?"

The boy curls his lower lip and shrugs.

"Loud enough, I guess."

Richard Blyth, Harper's older brother and the senior member of the firm, is sitting on a couch in our office's waiting room, drinking coffee from a Styrofoam cup. He has a magazine butterflied open across his lap and when I walk in he looks up and nods.

"Good morning, Gordon," he says, taking a long swallow from his cup.

I smile and pass, plucking two yellow message slips from the rack beside our secretary Mary's desk.

"Wait, I'm just finishing another," Mary says. She puts down her pen and waves the ink dry before surrendering the slip. "It's from Joyce Ives. She also called right after you left last night, said she was going to get you at home."

"She didn't."

"Good," Mary says, folding her arms across her chest. "She sure can be bothersome."

I tell Mary she is right and then head down the hallway, peeking into Harper's office. He is on the phone, but he motions me in, raising an index finger to let me know that he'll only be a minute. On the far wall, there is a framed painting of a girl lying alone in a large maize-colored field. Harper had a similar print hanging above his bed in law school, and whenever I went over to his room, I imagined that the picture must be what Kansas looked like—that it reminded Harper of home. But, actually, Kansas doesn't look much like the picture at all. At least not the parts of Kansas I've seen. Kansas is not nearly as flat, and it's a lot greener.

Harper hangs up the phone and then leans back into his chair, locking his fingers behind his head.

"I want you to do something for me," he says. "I want you to take Joyce Ives's case."

My lungs fill several times before I respond. "We talked about this. As a matter of fact, you're the one who told me that I'd be crazy if I *did* take it."

"I know, I know. But do me this favor: call her—talk to her. Tell her you'll take it."

"Harper, you know this case? She's insane. Her husband was cheating on her with a waitress at Gooland's, so Joyce followed him there, on his lunch hour or something, and then drove her car through the fuckin' front of the restaurant. Not only is she *not* willing to pay for the damages she caused to Gooland's—which, I understand, is in the neighborhood of twelve thousand dollars—but she's suing to recoup her costs for the crushed car *and* for money she spent on hospital bills. From what I hear, she suffered a pinched nerve in her neck and lacerations to her face when a couple of cinder blocks shattered her windshield."

Harper removes a cigar from a polished mahogany humidor on the corner of his desk. He pulls a black clipper from his top drawer and snips off the end of the cigar, brushing the thumbnail-sized nub onto the floor.

"This is not a good case," he says, rolling the cigar against the center of his tongue, forming a saliva-filled trough. "I am certainly aware of that. But do this for me. I have my reasons."

"Are you going to tell me what those reasons are?"

Harper holds the cigar gently between his teeth, moving the flame of an orb-shaped lighter toward the blunt tip.

"I will," he answers, making the word "will" sound more like "with" as his tongue knocks against the soft butt of the cigar. "Just not yet." His face disappears behind a funnel of smoke and I move toward the doorway, turning back before I leave.

"What's your brother doing in the waiting room?" I ask.

"He's reading. Buster Horry complained to him the other day about our assortment of magazines, said there were too many for women. Richard said they were divided evenly, fifty-fifty. But it seems Buster categorizes any publication that doesn't solicit advertising for manure spreaders as being for women."

An enormous piece of clear plastic is held by uneven sections of silver duct tape over the outside wall of Gooland's. It shields a hole roughly the size of a Dodge Dart. A small piece of the plastic is dog-eared above the upper left-hand corner, winking in the breeze. High, away from the damage, a wooden sign spells out Gooland's vertically, from top to bottom, in red block letters. At its base, in horizontal blue cursive, it says: Breakfast Served Anytime. Inside, a space heater rests beside the unwanted opening, its coil red-faced and throbbing. A long linoleum counter bisects the far end of the restaurant, behind seven swivel-top stools. Eight tables are pressed tight against the side walls—four on each side—and six more tables are arranged about center-floor. Squeezed into white polyester, a waitress leans against the cash register while leafing through the newspaper. Only a couple of the tables are occupied.

I sit at the counter and another waitress appears from the kitchen. She is wearing the same dress as the first waitress, but she has a thick cardigan sweater overtop.

"Coffee?" she asks.

I nod and place my briefcase on the stool at my right.

"Eggs are good today. The new grill's just broken in," she says, placing a saucer and cup in front of me and filling it with coffee. “For the first few days everything tasted sort of funny—metallic.”

She sets a folded napkin on the counter. “Let me get you some silver. We just did a set.”

My father ate breakfast most mornings of his adult life in a diner much like Gooland's. It was perched on a sleepy ridge overlooking Lake Erie, and on more than one occasion I heard him say to Sara, the restaurant's proprietor and chief cook, that the best thing that could happen to the old place was for it to crumble off the side of the earth and dissolve into the lake. After hearing this, oftentimes Sara would come out from behind the plasterboard wall that separated the kitchen from the eating area, and shove my father against the inside of his corner booth. She would settle down next to him, her apron hiked up above her dimpled brown knees, and explain why it wouldn't do to have her restaurant resting beneath the waves. She would always finish by saying, “ 'Sides, Hap, if this place wasn't here, you'd have nowhere to go.”

The waitress comes back, wiping the silverware dry with a cloth napkin before laying it out. I stir cream into my coffee with the still-warm teaspoon and ask to see the manager.

“Is there something wrong? You ain't had nothing but coffee.”

“No, everything's fine. Business.”

Frankie Larch is tall with stooped shoulders and a narrow, crooked spine that cups slightly below his neck. He comes out from a small office behind the kitchen and takes the stool at my left, swinging his long legs away from the counter and into the center of the restaurant. He is wearing a newly pressed blue button-down and khaki slacks that pull up an inch or so too short. He touches a lonely patch of stubble at the base of his chin, brushing it with his fingertips as if willing it to expand and cover the rest of his face.

"Gordon," he says, nodding. "I knew you'd be out here sooner or later. She told me you'd probably be handling this for her."

I shrug and turn to retrieve my briefcase.

"Hey, I understand it's only business. So I won't hold it against you. But to be perfectly honest, I don't think you're gonna do too well with this one."

"You know, Frankie," I start, removing a yellow legal pad. "I think a lot of people feel that way."

Frankie inherited the restaurant from his mother, Ellen Gooland. He has been running it pretty steadily for nearly ten years without much trouble, until Joyce Ives. The two of us get up and move over to a side table, the waitress bringing me a fresh cup of coffee and Frankie a glass of Pepsi.

"Rob was seeing one of my waitresses—Carol," Frankie says, looking over his shoulder. "She ain't here now. But Rob had been coming in real regular during her shifts, for about six months or so. I figured everyone knew—I mean, it's not like they acted hush-hush. Christ, I saw them holding hands a bunch of times. They even kissed each other goodbye—depending on who was around."

"Did you ever say anything to Carol?" I ask.

"Naw. It's none of my business who she sees and

who she don't. As long as she shows up on time and does a good job."

Frankie removes a pack of Marlboros from his shirt pocket and offers me one, lighting both cigarettes with the same match. I inhale deeply and after several seconds begin to feel a rush.

"So, tell me about that afternoon."

"Well, there ain't really all that much to tell. I was standing"—he pauses and turns, pointing toward a glass case beside the cash register that holds mostly chewing gum, candy bars, and cheap cigars—"there. I remember I was talking to Kyle Freeder about this new television set he got. And all of a sudden I hear this grinding noise—actually, it was more of a scraping. Like a snow-plow on hard pavement. After that, the whole wall comes in with the front end of her Dodge."

"And then what happened?"

"Before or after Rob pissed in his pants?" Frankie says, grinning. "No. Really, I'm not sure. I remember Joyce getting out, real calm-like. At that point I thought she might have had an accident, that something may have gone wrong with the car. But it was pretty quiet." He lights another cigarette with the stub of his last. "You could hear some pieces of glass falling and things settling, but it was basically quiet. Joyce walked over to Rob, plain as pancakes, and said, 'I saw you from outside.' She handed him the keys and said, 'You can drive it home, when you come to get your things.' And that's it. She turned and left—Rob just standing there with the car keys hanging from his finger."

I sigh, clipping my pen to the legal pad and returning them both to my briefcase.

"There were a good many people in here. We're real lucky no one was hurt."

I thank Frankie for his time and slip a dollar underneath my coffee cup. Outside, the sky has started to clear and the air is warming—a final feverish cough before fall. Frankie follows me into the doorway, leaning down to switch off the space heater.

I fold my suit jacket over the passenger seat and sit still for a few moments, hand atop the stick shift, keys in my lap. Jiggling the stick, I practice sliding it down toward reverse.

TWO

Calvin is sitting on the front staircase of the Coopers' house, his head settled deep between his knees. Charlotte is behind him, husking corn and piling it neatly at her side. As I pull in, she stands and taps Calvin on the back of his head before moving down the stairs and onto the dirt and gravel driveway. She comes over to my side of the car and I roll open the window.

"Meg is sick," she says, crouching, resting her elbows and forearms against the car door. "I don't think it's anything serious, but I decided to keep them apart. To be safe."

"Thanks."

Calvin creeps in behind Charlotte and then jumps up, growling, his hands forming claws at both sides of his face. A section of orange rind is pressed against his teeth, between his gums, and when he makes his growling noise it starts to slide loose, forcing him to take down one of the claws and adjust his soggy fangs.

"And what is this?" I ask, shutting off the engine.

"Charlotte, I leave my only son with you and he turns into a lion."

Calvin straightens, spitting the orange cuticle into the dirt. "I'm *not* a lion, Dad. I'm a saber-tooth tiger."

"Geez, Gordon. Don't you know a saber-tooth tiger when you see one?" says Charlotte.

"Hmmm. I guess not. I mean, it's been a while."

Calvin retrieves the dirt-covered orange, but Charlotte takes it away before it hits his lips. He whines, reaching as Charlotte moves it to her chest.

"Unh. I want it."

"This one is yucky, Cal. We'll get you another," says Charlotte, folding the rind into her breast pocket.

"That's okay," I say. "Maybe tomorrow—if Meg is better. Let's go, Cal."

"This side," he says, flexing his fingers toward the open window. I know what he means and hang my left arm out for him to grab. When he has a hold, I hoist him in through the window and across my lap to the passenger seat.

"Thanks, Charlotte. I'll call you in the morning."

Charlotte stands with her arms crossed low, above her stomach. As we back out she waves, first big and then with only her fingers, for Calvin. Calvin sits up on his knees and waves, too, following Charlotte from the front windshield to the side and finally out the back.

"How do you feel, fella?"

Calvin turns and sits down, kicking his legs out from beneath. I lean in and pull his seat belt over-top, struggling one-handed with the buckle.

"Can you give me a hand here?"

He takes the chrome end from me and plunges it into the receptor, waiting for me to sit straight. When I do, he hits the button and flicks the belt free, banging it against the dashboard and then the door.

"Hey, that's not funny. Fix it."

He yanks the seat belt back from behind his waist.

"Okay, now fasten it and leave it that way."

He does.

"So, I asked you a question."

"Huh?"

"How do you feel?"

"Meg's got a cold," he answers, pointing the toes of his sneakers toward the radio.

"I know she does. That's part of the reason I'm asking you."

"I feel fine."

"Yeah, well, I wouldn't be the least bit surprised if you did come down with something—the way you went out this morning."

"How?"

"Going after Moonie in just your pajamas. That's how you catch cold."

"Did Meg go out in her 'jamas?"

"I don't know."

"Well, she's got a cold."

I twist my head, shooting him a wry look. But he is propped up against the door, peering out the window.

"Hey, how 'bout we listen to the radio?" he says.

"What do you want to hear?"

He shrugs, pushing his head back into the soft middle portion of the seat. I turn on the radio, leaving it on a classical station he usually likes. Not so much for the music, but because of the disc jockey's deep, soulful voice.

"No, not this."

"What's wrong? Wait a minute, you'll like the guy who talks when the music ends."

"*Nooo*. I don't like him anymore."

"Sure you do," I say, turning up the volume. "Wait. He'll be on in a second."

Calvin tries to stretch forward to change the channel, but he cannot reach. He starts to grab at the seat buckle.

"Don't!" I say, spreading my hand across his chest. "I'll try something else if you can ask in a nice, polite way."

"Could we hear another music?" he says.

I shake my head and he sighs, real loud, inadvertently spitting saliva onto his pants. He is thinking.

"*Please*, could we change?"

I am tempted to tease him, but I do not, instead switching to a fast-paced top-forty station. When I stop, he smiles and says, "Yeah, this." We pull leisurely into a parking lot beside the post office.

"What're we doin' here?" he asks, climbing out of the car.

"I have to pick up a package before they close."

"What package?"

They are not crowded inside and only one window is in use. I surrender my pink slip and the man behind the counter tells me to wait.

"What are you getting?" Calvin asks. He is now

standing on the balls of his feet, excitedly shaking his hands at his waist.

"I don't know."

The man places a tall, narrow package, wrapped in brown paper, on the countertop. He hands me a clipboard and pen and asks me to sign beside the bottom number, which is 39.

The outside of the box is covered with red scrawl, telling all who handle it to "Keep This End Up" and that its contents are "Extremely Fragile." I recognize the writing and the pen as belonging to my mother, who has sent this from Key Biscayne. Although it is addressed to me, enclosed in parentheses beside my name it says, "For Calvin." So I take him outside and the two of us sit on the steps of the post office.

"It's from Grandma Tish," I say, using my keys to slice a large H through the tape, where the flaps come free. "It's for you."

Calvin's head lunges forward and his eyebrows rise and then drop. "Dad, for me? You opened it," he says, with a tremor to his voice.

"No, no. Look, I just made it easier. I have no idea what's in here." I take him by the wrists, from behind, and push him toward the box. He leans over and begins ripping away at the cardboard, tape, and crumpled newspaper. He digs down, but is having trouble prying his gift loose.

"Unhh. It's heavy."

"Do you want help?" I ask, moving closer.

"No, I—I." He pauses and takes a full breath. This means, indeed, he would like me to get rid of all the excess packing materials so he can see his present. I place my hand into the box and pull out a thick, wobbly mason jar filled with saltwater, and floating, almost perfectly centered, a violet-blue handlike glob. I turn it and on the side, where a right-thinking person might label "Summer Peaches" or "Strawberry Rhubarb," my mother has written "Portuguese Man-o-War." She has sent my four-year-old son one, very much expired, Portuguese man-o-war.

Calvin is reaching, his eyes wide and warm, like cinders. I set the jar at his feet and tell him he can look, but not to touch it. I tell him they have laws in Kansas against little boys holding dead Portuguese man-o-wars —especially on the steps of the post office. However, he is not listening.

I take the empty box and newspaper to a large garbage bin several spaces away from my car and cram them inside, firmly, with both arms. Looking back, I watch Calvin, his hand waving in front of one side of the jar as he talks to the man-o-war. I cannot quite make out what he is saying, but I am sure he has had similar conversations with worms and slugs.

When I was young, my mother often attempted to bring bizarre presents home for me from trips. Most Christmases, my parents were away with the basketball team at a holiday tournament in Hawaii, California, or Florida. Always someplace warm. She would leave gifts behind for me to open with my grandparents, but she would also try to bring back something from the trip. I can only imagine my father's reactions as she attempted to stuff starfish wrapped in plastic sandwich bags into his suitcase, or when she was stopped by security at the Maui airport for carrying a package too large for the plane—a package that turned out to be a lobster trap. My mother told me later that my father asked her repeatedly what was I going to do with a lobster trap in Ohio. She responded by saying she thought it might be nice in my bedroom, that perhaps I could learn something from it. When my mother talks of these items, with hindsight, I believe it was the lobster trap that was the hardest for her to leave behind. Not so much for what it was, but for the manner in which it was abandoned.

The episode occurred in late December 1974, and Eastern Ohio was playing Michigan State in the final of the Maui Christmas Classic. The Eagles had won their first game, beating Hawaii–Loa by 62 points, and although Michigan State was a much tougher opponent, the two teams had played a month earlier, with Eastern Ohio winning by 16. Because of the time difference, television dictated the final begin at 10 a.m., which ripped my father. He detested catering to anyone, especially the "copper-fucks" at TV. But as the game started, my father seemed uncharacteristically relaxed, his legs extended, crossed at the ankles. He normally drank a pot of coffee a half, but here he was sipping a local brew of herbal tea from a cardboard cup. The game stayed relatively close until early into the second half, when the Eagles went on a 12–3 run and it looked as if Michigan State would collapse. With a little more than six minutes remaining, Eastern Ohio led by 14 and had possession of the ball. Really, it was an innocent mistake, a split-second decision gone wrong.

The play was called three-ramble: guard David Paccini was supposed to take the pass above the free-throw line and turn to face the basket; forward Harvey Brewer cuts off a baseline pick from left to right, and if he is open, Paccini gives him the ball; if he's covered, Paccini either kicks the ball back out top to the point guard, Mort Keane, or shoots. Brewer was not open, but Paccini forced the ball anyway and Michigan State stole it, pushing an outlet pass that keyed its fast break. As the Spartans closed the play with a lay-up, Paccini, desperately trying to make amends for his error—for now, out of the corner of his eye, he could see my father standing and yelling something at the referee—tried to block the ball and fouled the shooter. A three-point play.

My father erupted, but not at Paccini. He was busy riding the ref, believing the player who stole the ball had gone over Brewer's back to do so. The usual stream of profanity spewed from my father's mouth, his arms spread out, gesturing in front of him. My father had worked his way closer to the ref, almost touching him, and when the referee turned around, he hooked the cup of tea onto himself. Perhaps the referee truly believed my father had intentionally doused him, or maybe he just wanted to shut my father up, but the result was a technical foul. The Eagles' lead was cut to 9 and after two successive possessions that ended in missed shots, the margin was down to 5. Then my father called time, but instead of talking to his players, he continued shouting at the referee. Michigan State moved ahead for good with 1:32 left, and eventually won the game, 77–72.

At the airport, my father was quiet as the team passed through twin metal detectors. It was there that the security guards made my mother unwrap the lobster trap, and then an airline representative came over to inform her the piece would have to be checked: it was too large to carry on the plane. This was the first time my father had seen—or cared—what she was balancing against her outer thigh.

"Tish, why do you have this thing?" he asked my mother.

"For Gordon's room."

"Jesus, he doesn't need a lobster trap—that's what it is, isn't it? A lobster trap?"

"Well, I thought—"

"What the hell is he going to do with this?"

"Actually, it might be a nice teaching tool."

This was always my mother's escape. No matter how offbeat something was, it just might strike a chord somewhere inside my head or heart, and I would become ravenous for knowledge about starfish or lobster traps or seagull feathers, and this would pave the path to my future.

"Lobster trap," my father said, sighing. I believe all would have been fine if at that moment he had simply turned the other way and walked toward the airline gate, leaving my mother to repack and check her trap. But my father looked up and saw David Paccini leaning against the wall, his black hair slicked back, his right hand fiddling with something at his knee—the butt of a tennis racket. It took a minute before Paccini noticed my father was staring at him, but when he did he became rigid and uneasy. My father called Paccini over and asked him for the tennis racket, which he took to where my mother was standing. He pushed her off to the side and then folded the racket, six times, into the trap, leaving splintered shards of wood and random netting about the table and floor.

"It'll fit now," my father said, brushing off his shirt and waist. He walked back to Paccini, handing him the badly disfigured racket—head snapped free, clinging by a half dozen or so limp and twisted strands of cat gut.

"Here," he said, shouldering his carry-on bag. "If Brewer's not open, don't give him the ball."

There is almost daylight. Breathing easy, waiting for the wasp-buzz of the alarm clock, I think, it is mornings like these when Calvin needs another parent. A mother. The type of mother Kate was capable of being —if only demonstrated briefly. Early, when Calvin was still an infant, we took him along with us to an art museum. After we had seen acres of paintings and drawings by big names, like Picasso, van Gogh, and Matisse, Kate pushed Calvin's hooded carriage through one final room, a contemporary exhibit. Hanging from the ceiling at the far corner was a long, tubular punching bag with words stenciled on its swollen midsection. From afar, I watched as Kate wheeled Calvin around the bag in small circles, like heavy liquid swirling down a drain, reading to him from the piece of artwork.

It is a perfect instance—a complete moment between mother and child. One that cannot be scripted, but simply arises, quickly, and then disappears again. Kate and Calvin moving faster and faster, almost at dizzying speed until their two images blurred into one.

There were similar obscure moments between Kate and myself. The one that burns strongest happened shortly after we began dating. The two of us were early for a movie, so Kate took my hand and led me into a grocery store beside the theater. There, we roamed the aisles, pausing, randomly, so Kate could question me about various products. Actually, what she wanted was to rate the items in her favorite sections: "Pick your top three cookies" (mine: Oreos, Chips Ahoy, and Mallomars; hers: chocolate-covered graham crackers, Mallomars—common ground!—and Nutter-Butter peanut butter), or "One cereal to take with you on a desert island—prizes *not* included" (mine: Cocoa Krispies; hers: Raisin Bran).

Before leaving, we passed through the frozen foods and Kate reached for my arm while a Muzak mambo came over the speaker system. We held each other tightly, shifting on the balls of our feet. People glared at us, concerned, as they guided their carts past meat, frosty and cellophaned. Even here, even now, everything was possible. We could spend time in the Peace Corps, someplace exotic —Tibet, perhaps. We could live on beaches in faraway lands until we decided to settle down, and then we might choose the hills near Tuscany, raising our children to speak two, three languages. Or, maybe, we would decide that Eau Claire, Wisconsin, was just fine, too.

Still, I knew it would not always be like that—pure with potential. What you hope, I suppose, is that there are more days when the good will keep you buoyed than days when it will not.

Calvin is lying stomach-down across his bed, fists supporting chin. He is staring at the man-o-war resting atop the windowsill. A narrow bar of sunlight slides in through the cracked shades, breaking apart into glorious apricot and violet fingers as it hits the jar.

"Meg is still sick," I say, toweling off my hair. "And Mrs. Grafton's got plans today, so you're going to have to come to work with me."

He moans and curls his legs back, kicking at the seat of his pajamas with his heels.

"Hurry, and get dressed."

He lets out a long sigh, which, because his jaw is stable, sounds fleshy and spit-filled. As I head across the hallway, he calls out to me.

"What?" I answer, standing inside my door.

"Canya come here a minute?"

"Why?"

"I jus' wanna ask you something."

I walk back and he has not moved.

"Yes?"

"Do you think I should name my Poor'geese man-o-war?"

"Well, I suppose that's up to you."

"I think I'm gonna."

"Okay, that's fine," I say, grabbing his ankle and

sliding him to the end of the bed. "But right now you're going to get dressed."

I have fastened a wire coat hanger to the stainless-steel-clipped lid of the mason jar, creating a handle so Calvin can carry it. He holds it with both hands, slugging against the side of his calf and knee. Mary peeks up from her desk as we pass, craning her head to catch a better glimpse.

"What've you got there, Calvin?"

"It's a man-o-war," he says, resting the jar at his feet, but refusing to release the handle.

"Isn't that something. And where did you get him?"

"My gramma sent it—from Florida."

"Oh, that's nice," Mary says, looking at me with a bewildered, inquisitive expression.

"My mother's like that," I say.

"Does he have a name?"

"Not yet," says Calvin, guiding his hands evenly along the wire, like it's a steering wheel. "But I'm thinking of one."

"That's good. A man-o-war's got to have a name."

Calvin and I start down the hallway, toward my office, but as we get to the door he turns back at Mary.

"It's a Poor'geese," he says.

"Excuse me?" Mary answers, standing.

"He said it was Portuguese. The man-o-war. It's a Portuguese man-o-war."

"Oh, I see."

My office smells of Harper's cigars and I open the

window, as wide as it will raise. I slide my large leather chair, with rollers, around to the front of the room because Calvin likes sitting in it.

"Are you hungry?"

He shakes his head and then climbs onto the chair, trying to pull the jar up behind him.

"No. You'll break it. Leave the man-o-war on the floor."

His feet rattle toward the ceiling as he leans back deep into the high leather padding of the chair.

"Okay, I'm going to set you up right here," I say, taking a stubby end table and pushing it to his left. I pull open the drawstring on his gunnysack and set out two coloring books—one of dinosaurs, the other of race cars—a set of crayons and water-base markers, a wooden automobile, a thin hard-covered book about a little fireman, and a stuffed panda bear.

"I'm also putting this here, for when you're thirsty." I take a tiny apple-flavored-juice box and place it beside his truck.

"Uh, no," he says, clapping his hands. "I wanna do the straw."

"All right. I'll just leave it here and you can stick the straw in when you're ready."

Harper enters and stops behind Calvin, nudging at the chair with his knees. Calvin lets out a whine and looks up, backwards. When he sees that it is Harper, he settles on the chair's arm and bites his upper lip with his lower teeth, fang-like. Harper does the same thing, letting out snorting sounds that Calvin tries to match. It is their mutual greeting.

"You got your brain in that jar?" Harper asks Calvin, smirking.

"Nah." Calvin is laughing. "It's a man-o-war."

"Oh, really?"

Harper moves to the side of my desk, slipping a flimsy manila folder onto the blotter.

"Joyce Ives dropped this stuff off after you left yesterday." He breathes in, and looks again at Calvin. "Does your man-o-war do any tricks?"

Calvin nods. "Watch this." He turns the jar upside down and the man-o-war rights itself, and then floats to the inverted top.

"Neato."

"Not neato. Don't do that, Cal. All I need is for that thing to bust open and spill."

Calvin sulks, pursing his lips and squeezing his eyebrows close until they almost meet.

"What's in here?" I ask Harper, taking the folder and opening it.

"The accident report, along with copies of her last three auto check-ups."

"Lemme guess, brakes fine three times."

Harper shrugs and then kneels down near Calvin, tapping at his juice box. "You gonna drink this?"

"Yesss."

"Well, here," Harper says, lifting it and preparing to jab the straw through the tiny foil hole. "Let me help you."

Harper knows Calvin usually likes to do the straw part, and in an instant Calvin is up, tugging at one of Harper's belt loops.

"All right, all right. I'm just foolin'. Here you go."

Calvin takes the juice, along with his man-o-war, and slinks into a far corner, kicking off his sneakers and knocking them into the center of the room. I leaf through the folder, finding nothing much of interest.

"Zero."

"I know. Christ, she didn't even need wiper fluid." Harper steps over Calvin's shoes and back to the door, turning to Calvin before exiting, to shoot him the A–O.K. sign. Calvin covers his eyes with his inner elbow.

"You haven't talked to Joyce yet, have you?" Harper yells from his office.

"I'm saving her for last."

"Should do it soon." There is silence, and then Harper says, to no one in particular, "What makes people do these things?"

I have often wondered this myself. The thought seemed most relevant, however, when it concerned my father. One of life's great ironies, as I see it, is that my father was called Happy. Henry "Happy" Nash. He was given the nickname by his high-school basketball coach, who would always tell my father to smile, to at least pretend he was enjoying himself. Personally, I can recall seeing my father smile only four times in the twenty-seven years I knew him. Actually, I only remember three of those times, though I am told that his mouth did raise slightly at the corners after my birth. He grinned—beamed even—twice following basketball games: after a last-second overtime win at Notre Dame (most of this pleasure derived because Notre Dame would not accept my father when he was matriculating); and following a victory over UCLA for the national championship. The only other time was outside an Italian restaurant in Cleveland. The Eagles had just defeated Northern Illinois and my father and I were meeting my mother for dinner. As we got out of the car, my father took my shoulder and told me to wait by the curb. A stout, well-dressed man was standing in front of a green neon window sign, picking at his teeth with the edge of a business card. His suit was dark and loose-fitting, despite his substantial girth. He wore his tie low, with the top button of his white shirt unfastened. My father walked up and was immediately recognized.

"Hey, Happy. Long time." The man spoke quickly, in short staccato bursts. "Nice win tonight. Nice win."

By the time my father got close, I could see what he was going to do. He was going to hit the man. His right fist was clenched, and he reached up with his left hand and grabbed the man's tie, lifting it into his chin. The man pushed awkwardly at my father, trying to slap himself free. But his attempts were lame, almost childlike in their ineffectiveness. My father cocked and slugged the man high on the cheekbone, freeing him from his grip in the same motion. The man dropped to his knees, using the heel of his palm to dab at the spider of blood below his left eye. My father walked back to me and I noticed the knuckles on his hand were all red and puffy. As we headed toward the restaurant, my father told me that when we first moved to Lakeshire, while I was still an infant, that man had sold us some furniture. His name was Curtis Rhodes, and my father believed he had since left the home-furnishings business to try his hand at insurance. But on my father's second road trip with the Eagles, to Tucson and Salt Lake City, Curtis Rhodes called my mother and asked her out for drinks. She declined, and no matter how sincere Mr. Rhodes's intentions might have been, my father never forgave him. It was as we entered the restaurant, in the glow of the cigarette machine, that I could see my father smiling as he massaged the wrinkled edge of his right index finger.

It is unsettling for a boy to watch his father hit another man. Especially in the street, out in the open. In the moments before, everything moves slowly, like oatmeal. The motions seem contrived, heavy with anticipation. Once the punch is thrown, however, the softness no longer lingers. I could hear the muffled snap as my father slugged Mr. Rhodes and then a lumbersome *whumph!* when Mr. Rhodes collapsed, as if all the air had been pressed from his stomach and lungs. He sat hunched over for several minutes, feeling his face and mumbling in disbelief. The incident only helped smear that slender column between my father's own immortality and his stooped and weighted stature as a common man. An ordinary person. If my father could simply walk up to someone and hit him that easily, that effortlessly, then what was to prevent another man from doing the same to him.

Most of the afternoon I spend sorting through various legal volumes, attempting to find some loophole in Joyce Ives's case. For a moment I sit back and grin: it is such an odd little thing to choose to enter my brain. It was a strange event in the first place, something kindly Kate thought to do years ago—before we divorced, before, even, we married. I had been sick with fever and Kate sat beside me, in bed, blotting my forehead with a cold washcloth. Whenever she moved, I could feel the coarse hair of her legs rake against my hand.

Sometime during the night, delirious, I mumbled into her ear words about a rodeo: a *yellow* rodeo. Early the next morning, Kate asked me about it. I told her that when I was young I had these mysterious dreams: old Western dreams about rodeos where everything—horses, cowboys, fences, six-shooters—was yellow.

That afternoon, Kate woke me with a tray of chicken broth and carrot juice.

"It's on," she said, talking to a place above my shoulder.

"What? What's on?"

She walked to the television set and turned to a cable sports station showing a tape-delayed broadcast of the national rodeo championships in Omaha. Then Kate propped me against the wall with pillows and slid a pair of paper glasses—the kind people wore for 3-D movies—across the bridge of my nose. Covering the eye slits, though, was yellow cellophane that Kate had stapled at the corners.

"There you go, mister man. A yellow rodeo."

She fed me soup and then carrot juice, through a

straw, and together we watched a yellow rodeo—each taking turns with the crinkly glasses.

Calvin's day is also spent killing time; he eats his lunch—a peanut butter sandwich, Cheez Curls, and a banana—in the waiting room while leafing through magazines. Mary has shown him the Xerox machine and they make copies of his hands, left cheek, sneakers, and the bottom of the man-o-war jar. As I start to pack my briefcase with things to take home, Calvin steps into the doorway.

"Here," he says, surrendering one of the Xeroxed copies of his spread-open hands. "Mary said you'd like this."

"She was right. Come here."

I lift him onto my lap and lay the paper over a book on my desk. "Why don't you sign it."

He is still unable to write many things, but he can manage his name with help.

"What color," I ask, opening his box of markers.

"Red."

"Okay, red it is."

"No. Purple."

"Okay, purple."

We spell out his name in crooked, wandering purple, with a large C and an I that collides with the N. I take it from him and tape it low on my wall, beside a framed print by a local artist.

"Looks wonderful."

His chest swells with a tiny pride, and then he loses interest and grabs for his man-o-war. I fill his gunnysack and walk with him to the doorway, surveying the room one last time for anything we may have forgotten.

"You know somethin'," he says, resting the jar on his feet.

"Hunh?"

"I have a name for my man-o-war."

"That's great. What is it?"

"I'm gonna name him after Mom."

A warm, musty shaft of air blows into the room from a vent adjacent to my shins. After a few seconds it stops and Mary yells out an apology, saying she hit the wrong button.

"Hmm," I say. "I think that's nice. Kate is a beautiful name."

"No, not Kate. Mom."

"You want to call your man-o-war Mom?"

"Uh-huh."

"Well, Calvin," I say, setting my briefcase down and squatting on top of it. "That's nice. But—see." I am not really sure what to tell him, why something like this is not done. I do not have an answer, at least not one that a four-year-old boy will understand. And then it occurs to me if he truly wants to call his man-o-war Mom, that would be just fine.

"Okay. Mom then."

We sit for a moment in the car before leaving and he takes a blue crayon from his box, turning the immense mason jar between his legs. He marks his personal hieroglyphics on the corner of the label, above the word "man-o-war." I can make out the letter C and a backward R, but nothing else.

"There," he says, tongue pawing at the corner of his mouth. "Mom."

"Mom," I repeat.

A wiser father, a more compassionate father, might discuss the naming process in further detail with his son: analyze why, of the near-endless supply of names, Calvin selected Mom. However, I am not such a man. Rationalization is raw. It strikes me that in Calvin's tiny brain the notion of naming his dead man-o-war Mom had no more significance than calling it Scott or Beth or Peach or Blue. He does not miss this woman, I tell myself. How could he? The only mother he knows, *really* knows, is Charlotte—and, of course, Moonie the cat.

The sun settles into the horizon, showing only its top half, like some enormous nuclear umbrella. Chalky clouds are rolling in from the west, their undersides black and thick with rain.

"Mom." Calvin whispers to himself, touching the end of his nose with his index finger.

THREE

Mercer Street runs four lanes wide through the center of Tarent, moving east and west. About a half mile outside of town, in both directions, it becomes only two lanes. At its roomiest stretch, Mercer is cradled by buildings of white clapboard and dull, grainy brick, never rising more than five stories high. There is a supermarket with foot-long red Plexiglas letters, mounted directly onto its brick façade, spelling out Stop 'n' Shop. Its windows are thick and grimy, mostly covered with taped-on signs announcing daily and weekly specials on items such as paper towels, canned pinto beans, Tastee Tabby cat food, and lime Popsicles (in season). To one side of the market is an office building that houses a State Farm insurance agency on the ground floor and a chiropractor and a tailor on the second level. Beside that, a men's haberdashery where I have purchased a number of items, including two suits: a dark navy wool and a tan gabardine; several ties; socks; underwear; and a set of braces that I rarely wear.

On the other side of the market is the smaller of Tarent's two pharmacies. Ryder's is narrow, with an inlaid tile floor and a long, polished oak-and-brass soda fountain. Supplies are still shelved high and steep, with two thin roller-mounted ladders to reach them. At the far east corner of town, just as you enter, is Metro Drug: a cavernous, modern discount store glowing blue with fluorescent light.

Across the street from Ryder's is a smoke shop that in addition to stocking a large variety of cigarettes and cigars, both domestic and foreign, sells newspapers, magazines, and a selection of board games. Most afternoons, there is a young Native American boy, about sixteen, who plays all comers at a chess set near the front window. When there is no one else around, he plays against himself.

There are two traffic-light intersections three blocks apart in the downtown spread of Tarent. Just beyond the second light, moving west, is an unpaved side street called Basco Road, where our law office is perched up a short, stiff staircase, on the walkway level. A lonely swatch of low, hard grass sits out front, hinged by an L-shaped flower bed growing morning-glories, chrysanthemums, and roses, which usually are picked early, for someone's sweetheart. Near the end of the building is a small patch of parsley that Mary cultivates for salads and cooking. The glass door at the front has Blyth & Blyth Law Offices stenciled above-center in white paint, with Richard's name below, then Harper's, and finally my own, painted on later in a slightly glossier white. Off to the right, if you are facing the building from the street, is a black-top parking lot with eight spaces marked out by narrow bars of yellow. Although the lot is never full, some of the spaces are reserved for the offices above ours, if Richard is able to rent them. In the farthest slot on the left, Rob Ives has parked his wife's Dodge. He is propped up on the trunk, his boot heels hooked to the fender, toes hanging over the edge. He is snipping callouses from his palms, using a fingernail clipper attached to a key chain.

Indeed, the front end of the car looks as if it has been driven through a cinderblock wall. The grille is badly twisted, caved deeply at the center, leaving its sides jutting out above the shattered headlights. Forming a rigid right-angled peak even with the tires, the hood has been smashed almost off its hinges, creeping up through the lower tier of windshield and onto the dashboard. On the right, an entire section of automobile has been removed above the wheel well, baring a steel-gray skeleton brushed lightly with the dander of rust. The same section on the opposite side is pressed tightly together, rippling softly like an accordion. Vertically bisecting the glassless windshield, a broom handle has been tied at both ends with burlap rope—one side to the driver's visor, the other to a wiper. Taped to the broomstick is the same thick transparent plastic that covers the outside of Gooland's, here guarding only the left side.

"I can't believe it drives," I say, walking toward Rob Ives.

"Sure. Not much wrong with the insides—as much

as she tried. Gets a little breezy, though," he says, briefly turning back to face the car.

Rob works for a Lawrence-based distributing company, delivering a wide range of products, from livestock feed to sour mash whiskey. Ever since the afternoon Joyce rammed into Gooland's, Rob has been driving the Dodge, and Joyce, his Camaro. He agreed to meet me here after dropping off his delivery truck, so that I could survey the damage.

"Don't know what you're looking for," he says, closing the nail clipper and dropping it, along with the keys, into his pocket.

"Nothing, really. I just wanted to see how badly it was damaged."

Rob nods and slides down off the trunk, pulling the cuffs of his trousers back over the tops of his boots. I move around the car, jotting the damage on a legal pad, pausing every few steps to take pictures with a Polaroid camera, collecting the snapshots beneath a clip at the top of my pad. Bending my knees, I crouch beside the missing section of car, craning my head underneath to get a better look. From the corner of my eye, I can see Rob smiling. We are not familiar, but I am sure he knows I have absolutely no idea what I am supposed to be looking for. Finally, I stand.

"Look all right?" he says.

"I suppose."

"Toldya, there ain't nothing much wrong with the innards. Nothing that wasn't messed up already."

"Like what?"

"Oh, no big deal. Sometimes has trouble turning over, so you gotta let it set awhile. That's 'cause it floods real easy. The steering also pulls a little to the left, mostly when you're stopping."

"Is that the brakes?"

"The drums wear a little unevenly. We have 'em sanded down every six months or so."

I open a folder in front of me, leafing through the tune-up records. "I don't see anything here that shows you get the drums sanded."

"Wouldn't be there. Joyce's brother usually does it, in Nebraska. We visit 'em a couple times a year and he always messes with her car. He's got his own tire-and-wheel place in Lincoln. Does it in an afternoon."

"When was the last time he looked at the car?"

"Oh, I guess it must have been May." Rob stops, scratching at his eyebrows with his forefinger. "No. We took my car up in May. Don't usually take the Camaro 'cause I don't want to put the miles on it. But this time we did, on account of I needed a new set of tires. Mark, that's Joyce's brother, he sells 'em to me at cost. So it must have been last December, for the holidays."

"You wouldn't happen to know his phone number up there?"

Rob shakes his head. "Got it at home, though."

"Could you call me with it, when you get a chance?"

"Sure." Rob shrugs. "But what do you wanna talk to him for?"

"I just want to check the brakes through him—that nothing could have gone wrong."

Rob covers his mouth with his right hand, brushing down several times, stopping before the end of his chin. He lets out a hard breath through his nose, causing his nostrils to flare. "Wasn't anything with the brakes, Mr. Nash. She just damn drove through the wall. Comin' for me."

"Why was that?"

"I know you know why," he answers, looking straight, not blinking.

"Because you were seeing one of the waitresses." I glance down at my legal pad for the name. "Carol?"

He does not respond for several minutes, standing rigid, hands quiet at his sides. "It's a queer thing. It wasn't like I was ever intending on seeing someone on the sly, you know? Me and Joyce was happy—geez! We still are, sort of. I love Joyce as much now as when we first got married. It ain't about that. It ain't about not loving her."

Rob takes several steps toward me and stops. I want to tell him that he does not have to go on, he can keep this to himself. But I don't.

"I used to think that Joyce was all there was for me, that we belonged together. I still kinda do. But . . . well." He looks to the sky, spreading out his fingers and running them back through his straggly brown hair. "I feel the same way with Carol. Like maybe there's not one or even two women out there that I'd be happy spending the rest of my life with. That maybe I could be just as content with someone else."

A soft ticking noise rises from the distance, like the

settling of an engine or a baseball card stuck in the spokes of a bicycle. But after several minutes it stops.

"You lose some of your desire for things, for people. There was a period of my life when I wanted only Joyce. But now I'm not so sure. I guess what I'm trying to say is that it's not about one perfect match. A person could have five, maybe five hundred, perfect matches. I just happened to run across two in my lifetime. Two at the same time."

Our living room smells horrible. Calvin is lying spread-eagled on his back staring up at the ceiling, the man-o-war floating beside his head. I lean close and sniff first Calvin and then the jar.

"The man-o-war reeks," I say, tapping Calvin's chest.

"Huh?"

"Your man-o-war is rotting. We've gotta get rid of it."

Calvin rolls onto his side and pulls the jar near to him, squeezing it between his stomach and thighs.

"Cal, can't you smell that?"

Mrs. Grafton walks in from the back porch, placing Calvin's gunnysack on a straight-back chair beside the doorway.

"I know, isn't it just awful?" she says, smoothing out the front of her sundress. "It's been like that all day. He wouldn't let me put it outside."

"We're throwing it away."

Calvin whines, kicking his legs against the floor,

which in his profiled state makes him look as if he is running.

Mrs. Grafton stoops down and strokes his cheek with her hand. "Come now, honey. Let's show your father what a big man you are."

He tucks his head against his shoulder and settles into a fetal position, folded like an omelet around the mason jar.

Mrs. Grafton steps back, pushing a strand of hair behind her ear. "This is so unlike him," she says.

"Oh, I wouldn't say that. He's got a pouty side, too. Don't you, Cal?" I ask, prodding at his ribs with the toe of my shoe.

He moans and then starts to cry, muffled at first and then louder, breaking into short gasps as he tries to catch his breath. The back of his green T-shirt wavers with each sob, holding thin shivers of light below the crease of his spine.

"This is quite distressing," Mrs. Grafton says, following me into the kitchen. I tell her it isn't, really. That in Calvin's four years of life I have spoiled him. He is far too accustomed to getting his way; he needs to learn things will not always work out for him. Even as I'm speaking this sentence, though, I realize how false and flat my words sound. Calvin, more so than most four-year-olds, more so than many adults, is aware of the fact that life is not always straight with us. For he has lost a mother. And at times is alone in a world he does not understand.

Mrs. Grafton collects her belongings, cradling them

near her breast as she steps onto the back porch. Moonie lies beneath a wicker rocker, remaining motionless even as the screen door slaps closed.

"Thank you," I say, unbuttoning the top of my shirt and loosening the knot on my tie.

"Oh, it's a pleasure. He's usually so good," she says, swallowing the hard consonant sound at the end. She turns and walks the seventy or so yards to her house. When she is nearly halfway, Moonie stretches and then taps quietly, effortlessly, down the steps and into the wake of Mrs. Grafton's path.

When I return, the living room is empty and I call out to Calvin, but he does not answer. I hear the pattering of his stocking feet on the floorboards above. I find him at the foot of my bed, huddled over the mason jar, which has been opened, leaving salty splashes beading on the dark brown floor. He is holding a blue bottle, its cap a marble at his side.

"What are you doing?" I ask. The air is terrific, sharp, but not only with the smell of the man-o-war. Calvin has poured cologne into the mason jar, spilling a salad-plate-sized ring onto the front of his shirt.

"See," he starts, standing. "It doesn't stink bad anymore. See. Smell."

I take the nearly empty bottle from him, screwing the top back on and buffing it dry with his shirt.

"And you think that's gonna do it?"

"Yeah," he says, his face shiny warm with excitement. "That's it. That's doin' it."

"Think so, huh?"

He nods and then steps back as I refasten the lid to the mason jar.

"Yeah. That's doin' it," he repeats, sincere as a sunrise.

The light begins as tight rows of glowing white coins, slowly dispersing into grainy wedges that meld together before they reach the perfect rectangle of green, making it impossible to tell where one beam starts and the next finishes, unless you follow the nearly seamless trails back up to their origin. The green is fierce, without variation, so hard it creates wavering bars of black against your eyes if you stare too long. Huddled to one side is a grandstand, wide and steep, of silvery cast iron and stiff planks of red-painted wood. There is a similar, smaller version of the grandstand at the opposite end, for fans of visiting teams. Calvin and I sit at the top, near the home team, so he can see, our lower backs pressed against a creaky rail for support. We are eating hot dogs wrapped in wax paper, and potato chips, which I have spread out on napkins between us. A jumbo-sized Pepsi sits at my side, away from Calvin, to avoid mishaps.

Tarent High's players are in helmets of muted gray with a thin red line down the middle and the red silhouette of a Trojan on both sides. Their jerseys are crimson, with black-and-white stripes on the sleeves and white numbers sewn to the front and back and on the shoulders. White three-quarter-length pants have a single crimson stripe down the sides. Most are wearing black cleats, but a few have on white, and Calvin points to them while kicking his own white sneakers out in front, at a right angle. From what I am told, Tarent has never been particularly good in football, with last year's team going 5–4, the third best record in school history. However, this season they are without their top six players from a year ago, all of whom graduated. So there is not a great deal of interest for this game, with Lawrence's North Bedor. Mostly parents of players, girlfriends, teachers, and a handful of students with nothing better to do on a Friday night. Calvin and I have several sections to ourselves and sometimes, in between bites of hot dog, he climbs down a few rows and sits, chewing, punching at his thighs to the rhythm of the marching band's bass drum.

North Bedor, in white and green, is both physically larger than Tarent and greater in number. The Grizzlies, as they are called, force Tarent into a turnover on the third play of the game—stripping the ball from a Trojan running back and carrying it down to the 14-yard line. Two plays later North Bedor's quarterback sails a perfect spiral to his tight end in the left corner of the end zone. The opposite grandstand shakes with green and white. High-kicking cheerleaders wave flimsy pom-poms of shredded crepe paper, fastened to the end of cigarette-thin sticks. One cheerleader back-flips her way to the edge of the playing field, where she stands and pauses, chest out, straightening the pleats in her skirt, before skipping back to the sideline.

"You like her?" I ask Calvin. He does not answer; he does not know what I am talking about. Climbing back toward me, he leans down and places both hands around the mouth of the flimsy Pepsi cup. I hold the bottom, helping him lift it to his face. Flecks of wax float on the liquid's dark, oily surface. Calvin takes large, open swallows that cause his Adam's apple to throb, pushing against the soft, taut skin of his throat. When finished, he pants, lips parted so he can catch his breath.

At halftime, Tarent is behind, 24–6. Richard Blyth comes over and stands a few rows below us, his right leg propped the next level up, his forearms crossed against his knee. Richard's oldest son, Sam, is a third-string wide receiver for Tarent. He is only a sophomore and still quite skinny and gawky. Richard asks Calvin if he is enjoying the game, if someday maybe he wants to play football. But Calvin is quiet, scribbling on a game program with my felt-tip pen.

"I think I may have rented the floor above us," says Richard.

"That's great." I'm watching a group of teenagers gathered at the bottom of the grandstand, in front of the black cinder track that encircles the field. "To whom?"

"A couple of accountants. They're kids—just outta college. Kansas State. One of them grew up around here. He says the other fella is from Tulsa. They're going to talk it over, but I've got a good feeling."

The teenagers' voices carry and I can hear them talking about a party later this evening at a Jake somebody's house. His parents have gone to visit relatives in Missouri and won't be back until late Sunday. One girl, dressed in a faded, oversized jean jacket, khaki trousers rolled up to midcalf, and high-top sneakers with red-and-gray laces, lets out a loud scream. Shaking her head, she grabs the arm of the girl next to her and shouts "No way" three or four times.

"Young business types are just the kind of people we want in there," says Richard. "Quiet. Responsible. Courteous."

A tall, blond-haired boy in a Tarent letter jacket walks up to the group. He is greeted by a girl in a blousy white turtleneck, speaking in rapid sentences that I cannot understand. She is using her hands, pointing beyond the craggly line of treetops, to her right. She brings her hands together, forming a T, and the blond boy nods, saying, "Second house."

"Are you going to get the price you wanted?" I ask Richard.

"I lowered it a little. They're just starting out and all and I figured I'd give them a break. But only until they get settled—six months or so. Then the lease goes back up to my asking price."

It has become breezy and I slip a sweatshirt on Calvin. He fights it at first, hooking his arms against his chest, folding forward, level to his legs. I rub my knuckles down the side of his rib cage, gaunt and exposed, causing him to giggle and squirm. He relaxes and I tug the shirt down over his head, pulling his arms out and rolling the sleeves back above his wrists.

The two teams return to the field in a trot—Tarent's limp and measured. Calvin stands high on the seat, stretching his neck as if looking for somebody. But he knows no one, at least not well enough to recognize unless you were to point them out and say their name. I grab hold of Calvin's jeans, my fingers buried inside the waistband near the small of his back. He slaps at my hand, moaning, while he tries to shove me away.

"You wanna fall?" I ask, jerking him from side to side.

He nods.

"Oh yeah?" I push him forward, dangling him horizontally over the seats in front of us. He laughs, waving his arms in a crawl stroke toward escape. Swimming to freedom. "You are a very peculiar boy," I say. Richard smiles slow and then turns, in time to see Sam glancing up in his bright, unsoiled uniform, the number 88 wrapped to his sides, the front and back ends tucked below his arms. Richard waves and Sam starts to wave back, but stops, looking around before lifting his hand quickly, lamely, wiggling his fingers and then reaching to snap his chin strap in the same motion. His helmet is too large and as he pushes the buckle into the right side, the helmet shifts against his head, lurching leftward.

"Well, I'd better be getting back," says Richard, pointing across the grandstand to where his wife and some friends are sitting.

"If it stays like this, maybe the coach will put Sam in."

Richard raises his eyebrows and shrugs. He says "Maybe" and then descends to the walkway at the grandstand's base, passing the group of teenagers as he returns to his seat.

My memories of football games with my own father are surprisingly pleasant. Sunday mornings I would awaken in time to read through the sports page while my mother prepared our lunches: three sandwiches apiece, usually kosher salami and Swiss cheese on Italian bread, an apple or pear or banana, cookies stored in plastic sandwich bags, pretzels—which my father preferred infinitely to potato chips—several cans of ginger ale, and a thermos of coffee. Game time was one, but we always left the house by eleven. With traffic, it took about forty minutes to get to the stadium and another fifteen minutes to park. We always took the same route: down Chester, right on East 9th, and then left to St. Clair, to the second of two underground parking garages.

We did not speak much, my father and I, and when we did, it was invariably about something trivial, like how I was doing in school or a recent movie we both saw or why the Cleveland Browns should or should not trade a particular running back or linebacker. It always seemed odd to me that my father, who made his living teaching, communicating, was unable to do so away from the game of basketball, with his own family. Later in life, after I had married, my mother told me that when she started dating my father, while they were both still in college, they would often stay up talking until five in the morning at a local doughnut shop. She would always be the one to break off conversation, say it is time to go, she needed sleep. When I asked her what they talked about, she took a breath, low and swift, and then said, everything. They talked about everything. I told her I found it hard to believe, and she agreed. It seemed like another lifetime, she said, or maybe one that belonged to somebody else.

Tarent has lost by 32 points. Sam Blyth played the last offensive series of the game, but the ball was never thrown in his direction. Calvin is tired and I carry him over my right shoulder, like a sack of grain. At our car, I watch the tall blond boy in the letter jacket talking with another girl, helping her into his pickup truck. A pair of miniature basketball sneakers hang from his rear-view mirror, red and black and white, swinging in quick ovals that change motion with the truck's movements. He rolls down his window and stops, exchanging words with another letter-jacket-clad boy before pulling out of the parking lot and onto Montgomery Street. As I lower Calvin to the seat, a woman's hand reaches in and brushes a gentle tongue of hair from his forehead. It is Joyce Ives.

"Hello, sweetie," she says to Calvin. Dressed in a tan hunting jacket and jeans, Joyce turns away, taking a cigarette from her purse. She touches its end with a silver Zippo and returns the lighter to one of the baggy pockets on her jacket.

"You caught us leaving. He's tired." I close Calvin inside the car, his head droopy as a daffodil.

"You're a hard man to get ahold of."

"I'm sorry. I've been kinda busy lately. How're you feeling?"

"I'm fine. Took the neck brace off two days ago."

"Really, I've been meaning to call you."

She nods, blowing cigarette smoke quick, like steam, from the corner of her mouth. "I heard you met with Rob."

"Yeah, but just to look at the car. To see how bad the damage was." I kick at some gravel, forming a small pile with the instep of my foot. "Rob says it's running pretty well."

"That's because I took my foot off the gas."

"Excuse me?"

"I took my foot off the gas—after I hit. That's why I didn't do more damage to the car or the inside of Gooland's. Shit, I could have driven right into the kitchen—with Rob as a goddam hood ornament."

I am not sure what to say, how to respond to Joyce. Staring down, I bury my toe in the center of the gravel pile and dig out a hole in its center.

"You wouldn't have really wanted to hurt him?"

"Maybe."

She tilts her head back, smoke clinging to her face as it lifts upward. Someone is playing country-and-western music on a radio and it gets softer as his car becomes more distant.

"Oh, heck. No. No, I didn't want to hurt Rob bad. Just scare him a little. Scare him a lot. And knock him on his ass."

We both smile. I walk around to the driver's side of the car, picking at a crusted stamp of bird dropping on the door handle with my key.

"Joyce, we're going to have to settle this whole thing away from court. Sit down, first with Rob and then with

Frankie Larch. You're not exactly in a position of power."

"Correct me if I'm wrong here, Gordo. But you're *my* lawyer. You're supposed to please *me*."

I don't like people calling me Gordo. Some of my father's friends used to call me Gordo, usually followed by a flat slap delivered between my shoulder blades. "Howya doin', Gordo?" But it sounds severe, more condescending, in the high, clean tone of Joyce's voice.

"Listen, I'm tired. Calvin is tired. He's not used to being up this late. Yes, you are correct, I am your lawyer. I didn't choose to be, but Harper asked me to take this . . . this . . . this case—for lack of a better word. If you want, we can plead temporary insanity or something. But nohow, in no universe, are you going to see one penny from anyone other than Rob."

Joyce rests her chin on the roof of the car, and when she starts to talk, she looks like a puppet. "We can sue him."

"For what?"

"For fucking around on me. For screwing some waitress behind my back."

"Jesus, Joyce." I open the door, grabbing at the top of the steering wheel, preparing to pull myself in. "You're married to the man. You know what he makes, what he has. You want his Camaro? You've already got it. What else, huh? What else is there?"

There is nothing else, really. The mortgage on their house cannot be worth much. Neither can his savings account.

"We can talk more about this next week," I say. "I

don't know what Harper has said to you, but your expectations are unrealistic. The best thing for everybody is to just sit down and talk this out."

She does not say anything for several minutes and I settle into the seat, sliding the key carefully into the ignition. Finally, she moves to the front of the car, dragging her finger along its dusty surface as she goes.

"He's living with her now," she says, loud, making sure I can hear her from where I'm sitting. "He's my husband and he's living with another woman."

I nod, as if I know how she feels.

She walks across the now empty parking lot into blackness and I watch her for a few steps and then start the car. When I look up, she is gone and it's too dark to find her again. A moment later, two car lights switch on and Rob's Camaro moves slowly toward the exit, gravel crunching beneath its tires. Squinting, I can barely make out the orange blush of a cigarette bobbing between Joyce's lips, as if she is talking to someone, but of course she is not. There is nobody with her, nobody at all.

Loy McLure is standing in a long white lab coat, arms crossed high against his chest, a stethoscope wrapped around his neck, its round, silver end tucked neatly into a breast pocket. His eyes are worried slits, dark pupils ticking back and forth, showing narrow milky petals on either side. He looks at me and then over to Calvin, who is perched on a light blue examination table, paper crinkling underneath his bottom. Loy walks to the sink and his shoes squeak as they lift from the tile floor.

"I'm not sure if this is going to work," he says, taking

out a gray plastic bottle. "The rot has already set in."

He leans over the brushed-steel counter, tapping at a strainer that holds Calvin's man-o-war. The man-o-war is the size of a fist, marbled, smooth, a translucent green speckling its underside. Mold, as on bread, grows randomly in several coin-sized blotches over its gummy skin. Loy spills alcohol on it and then half fills the mason jar with formaldehyde. When he sets the man-o-war into the jar, using rubber gloves, the formaldehyde erupts into small fizzing bubbles, hissing at the surface and then vanishing, sinking with its cargo.

"You'll have to wait and see," Loy says, pouring more formaldehyde into the jar, stopping a few inches before its top. "I don't know anything about these. This might make it worse."

He closes the jar and blots it dry with paper towels, handing it to Calvin, who grabs by the coat hanger. I tell him to hold tight while I lift them both to the ground.

"Where'd he get something like that?" Loy asks, peeling the gloves from his hands and dropping them into the trash.

"My mother sent it. From Florida."

"Sort of a peculiar gift, don't you think?"

"Yes. I do."

Loy nods, knowingly, as he takes out a box of Dum-Dum lollipops. Although Loy is only in his early forties, his hair, cropped short, is completely white. He is tall, healthy, with pink triangle-shaped patches following the bold angles of his cheekbones. Shaking the box, he tells Calvin to ask me if he can have one.

"Can I have a pop?"

I tell him he can, so he takes brown.

"That's root beer, Cal. I think you'd rather have cherry or grape," I say, reaching into the box and removing one of each. But he clings to the root beer, guarding it close to his breast.

Loy follows us out, through his empty waiting room and into the hallway, which is dark, drab, papered in green-and-black paisley. He asks me how Calvin and I are getting along, other than the man-o-war. We are fine, I say, bopping Calvin on the head with the pudgy heel of my fist. I thank Loy again, profusely, and apologize for taking up so much of his time, a statement he shrugs off.

Later, Calvin and I eat spaghetti for dinner. I cut his into inch-long pieces, but he complains, saying he hates it that way, refusing even a forkful. So I switch plates, instead giving him tangly, wig-like strands that whip up and slap sauce onto his cheeks. Our glasses are filled red, mine with inexpensive chianti and his with cranberry juice.

"It would be nice if you'd draw a thank-you card for Dr. McLure," I tell Calvin. "Or you could color him one of the pictures in your animal book."

"I'm keepin' that book."

"You can keep it. But maybe we could give one of the pictures to him. Don't you think?"

"No," he says, adjusting himself on the phone books that allow him to reach the table. Here they are thin, a paucity of names, so he needs three. Two white and a yellow. " 'Cuz then you'd have to tear it out."

"Yeah, but, Cal, it's only one page. Didn't you think it was kind of Dr. McLure to help you out—so we didn't have to throw away the man-o-war?"

He does not answer.

"Well, I'm leaving it up to you. But I'm going to be very disappointed if you don't do something for him."

Still, no response. He cocks his head slightly, to the left. I am annoyed because I really don't think he will do anything for Dr. McLure.

"You know what? I'm going to take this back to him." I lift the man-o-war jar from the chair between us, raising it like a trophy above my plate of diced spaghetti. Calvin slides down, running to my side, arms pointed stiffly upwards.

"Gimme it."

"Nope. I'm taking this to Dr. McLure and telling him to pour out all the formaldehyde he gave you. That you didn't appreciate it, anyway."

Of course, Calvin cannot reach the jar. He tries to climb onto my lap, but I scissor my legs, knocking him away. He becomes frustrated and panicky and starts crying.

"Now you're really not getting it."

After several more moments of tears, he steps back and then forward again, punching me in the thigh.

"Hey, that did it." I walk over to the door, Calvin now sprawled out on the kitchen floor, chest heaving. He knocks over a chair and then begins to wail uncontrollably.

"Okay, that's enough."

Placing the jar on the counter, near the window, I move back to Calvin. He kicks at me, wildly, and I grab his feet, holding them at arm's length.

"Calvin," I say, slowly, in a stern tone. "Stop."

He does not. So I yank him to his feet and smack him, solid, on his ass, which, strangely, causes his sobs to halt briefly before he runs from the room, crying even harder.

The dinner dishes cleaned and stored, I sit on our front porch and read the *Tarent Times*, the town's only daily newspaper. Most of the stories are national, taken from the AP or UPI wires. There is a serial killer in California, near Los Angeles, who stabs his victims in the throat with a six-inch ice pick and leaves Coca-Cola bottle caps over the bloody holes, earning him the nickname Coca-Cola killer. Hurricane Felicia is stalled a few hundred miles off the coast of Florida, trembling, preparing, and the United States Weather Service is quite sure she will slam into land, somewhere above Fort Lauderdale, within the next twenty-eight hours. They are hoping by then Felicia's winds will have diminished, pruning her to a tropical storm. Locally, a gooseneck trailer truck carrying several enormous elm trees from Montana jackknifed on Mercer, where it funnels into two lanes. A crew took four hours to lift the cab from its ditch, inching a chain and pulley rig, carefully, deliberately, so as not to snap loose the logs. There is also an announcement, boxed in the lower left corner of the front page, banning leaf burning.

It has turned breezy again and soon it will be winter. Our first full winter in Tarent. Mrs. Grafton is removing laundry from a clothesline she has strung between two thin poplars. The earth climbs, leaving the sun a smear of wax against the butterscotch stalks of wheat. Mrs. Grafton cannot see me now, it is too dark, too dark even for me to read. I am wearing a T-shirt and my arms are cold, so I cross them on my lap, sandwiching them between my belly and thighs. Calvin is no longer crying, or at least I can no longer hear him. It is very quiet, with only the sound of barn swallows, the light tap of wood against wood as Mrs. Grafton drops her clothespins into piles, and the occasional shush of a passing car.

Inside, I do not see Calvin. I don't want to see him because I am still angry, not only with him, but with myself. For overreacting. And for teasing him with the man-o-war, telling him that I was going to take it back to Dr. McLure. I read some more, in the living room, with a low-hanging floor lamp dispersing jaundiced yellow. After an hour I head upstairs, stopping at Calvin's room before retiring to my own. The only light is from the moon, coming in through the window, and I flip on a hallway switch. Calvin's animal coloring book is creased open near the center of the floor, to a picture of a hippopotamus, partially greened. His crayons and markers are scattered about, the farthest one, a burgundy, at the door. The bed is empty, stripped. I see his quilt, blue with astronauts and space ships, leading from the closet, where Calvin is lying face-down on the floor, sleeping, the quilt wrapped like a serpent about his body. Shoes and clothing rail a twisted pathway to a stuffed panda at his stocking feet. Calvin is making gentle noises, a soft, raspy snore rumbling from deep in his throat.

Because he is my son and because I love him more

than anything else in the world, more than I can imagine loving anyone else, more even than I loved his mother, I crawl in beside, my torso jammed deep into the closet, with my legs stretched over a hooked rug. I wrap my arm around Calvin, gingerly, and soon it tingles and becomes numb, but I do not move, leaving it resting over his tiny body like a wreath. Calvin's eyes flick, his wispy lashes brushing my cheek.

"Cal, how come you're sleeping in here?"

He is tired and answers slowly. "I just wanted to," he says, remaining still. "That's all."

Kate's labor was not a long one; it was not as excruciatingly painful as she expected, she told me later. Calvin came early, by almost a month, and I was in Cleveland at the time for my father's four hundredth coaching victory, an early February game against Stanford. The Eastern Ohio athletic department presented him with a plaque and gold watch at half court afterwards. Bruce Cutler, the school's sports information director, had a message on his answering machine saying that my wife's contractions had begun at 7:50 p.m., twenty minutes after tip-off. I received the news at 10:20 and left on a flight soon after, drinking watery Scotch from plastic cups the entire way. By the time I got to the hospital, in Ann Arbor, it was over. Kate was asleep.

She had been tucked in tightly, so only the peaks of her shoulders rose above the line of the blanket. Her round face smooth and bright, the silent mask of a worker. Freshly washed hair, light as split oak, spilled over the pillow, breaking slightly, delicately, as it dumped down on the mattress. I took her hand and lifted it to my chest and then my mouth, rubbing her fingers between my lips. I told her I was sorry I had not been there and that I loved her very much.

When I first saw Calvin, he was blotchy and red and I asked the duty nurse if he was okay, if he was supposed to be that way. She assured me he was fine, just fine, and I could hold him in the morning if I liked.

The hospital cafeteria was closed, so I sat in the doctors' lounge drinking vending-machine coffee. Kate's parents had not yet been notified. Her friend Denise left it to me. Denise had driven Kate to the hospital, had called Bruce Cutler's machine, had stayed with Kate until just before I arrived. Kate's parents could wait a few more hours, I remember thinking, and then I went back to her room. I climbed into bed beside her, squeezing close, my arms drawn across her chest like they are now against Calvin. The bed was short and narrow and sometime in the early morning I rolled off, cracking my face against the floor. My chin was sliced open, leaving a crescent-shaped flap dangling underneath my jawline. I stood in the bathroom blotting at it with clumps of Kleenex, toilet paper, and then a wet towel. There was blood sprayed over the front of my shirt, speckled and black. Shuffling, I made my way into the hall with a soppy towel clinging like a giant, distorted goatee.

Kate sat in a wheelchair holding my hand while they sewed eight stitches into my chin. She laughed a little and then told me about the delivery, about how easy things had gone. Then the two of us went to see Calvin. I cradled him carefully against my sternum while Kate ran her fingers along his mushy arm, and watched me.

I still had blood dried to my body and cheeks and a clean white bandage, thick with gauze, stuck to my chin.

Twenty-six months later, in our bedroom, I stood watching Kate. She was folding her clothes and stacking them into neat piles on the end of the bed.

"I was too young when we got married, Gordon," she said. "I still am too young."

We were married during the spring of Kate's senior year at Michigan, my second year of law school. She had wanted to be married—or to have a wedding, anyway. An event: white and pink and hers alone. And then she wanted a family. But she could close off her emotions with a simple, easy twist, like a faucet. Now it was time to get on with her future—the part that mattered. Calvin and I were baggage she could no longer tote. From us, she had graduated.

She told me she wanted to travel, to see more of the country, of other countries, that her father had offered to finance the trip. She was tired of Ann Arbor, of the people and of the town. She needed to be alone, away for a while, and then maybe things would change. In fact, she said she truly hoped they would change. Last, she volunteered to take Calvin, as someone might volunteer to take a pet, but she was not sure how much time she could spend with him. She believed he would be fine staying with her parents in Dallas. Thank you, I said, calmly, reasonably. He would remain with me.

That Sunday she left, driving the convertible BMW her father had given her after she finished school—weighted heavy with only the things she needed in her new life: skis, Walkman, a snorkel with which to breathe.

She had kissed Calvin goodbye twice, the second time on the stairs, telling him to be a good soldier and to listen to his father.

Earlier, because memories do not always follow a particular order, Kate said we had fallen out of love. I told her I had not, but she only nodded, saying I just didn't realize it yet. Love could be lost quickly, painlessly, and sometimes, she said, without one's knowing it.

Calvin stood in the window and watched her leave, waving his dumb little hand in a fury, as if she was only going on some vacation to see her sister or her aunt. After the car pulled from the driveway, free, she never once looked back, never saw Calvin still erect, his stupid, stupid hand moving faster, in shorter flicks. And I, too, had lost love. Quickly, painlessly, almost without knowing it. Then I took Calvin into the kitchen and fixed him a bowl of Lucky Charms soaked spongy in milk.

It is late and Calvin has turned away, his head resting against a crumpled baseball jacket. Again, the man-o-war is on the windowsill, blazing white in the moonlight, casting pale tiger stripes against Calvin's bed. I kiss him dryly on the ear and then stare up at the compressed row of his clothing hanging like fringe.

FOUR

Mom lasts another three weeks, until the middle of October, which was much longer than I expected. But the smell has gotten bad again, rank and oniony, and it is time she be given a proper burial. I tried to talk to Calvin about it, but he is indignant and will not listen, plugging up his ears and shaking his head whenever the subject is broached. And so I am parked at the entrance of Tarent's town dump with the man-o-war jar sitting on the seat beside me. The hollow, tinny sound of a hammer striking pipe echoes from somewhere inside the yard's tall, chain-link fence.

Just beyond the car, there is a gate that has been left open, with an enormous chain and padlock, fastened to itself, hanging off to one side. I take the man-o-war by the bottom of its jar, letting the now flimsy coat hanger dangle loose. The man-o-war sloshes about in its murky brine—broken shapeless pieces resembling a thick tangerine gelatin. I'm looking for serenity, a nice, nonthreatening spot where the man-o-war can decompose in peace. At the near edge of the fence there is a rusted-out car bumper propped between two tires that are worn so deeply, tiny wires have sprouted through their surfaces. Underneath the bumper is a Quaker Oats container, soggy and brown with age. This is where I pour the man-o-war, slowly at first, until wet clumps roll with force, slapping down like dough. As I stand, it becomes difficult to see the man-o-war, some of it vanishing into the Quaker Oats container, while the rest melts into earth.

After dinner last night, while Calvin helped Mrs. Grafton beat the dirt from her rugs using a small baseball bat, Kate called. Although it would have been easy for me to shout out to Calvin, to tell him that his mother was on the phone and he should come inside, I did not. I told Kate that he wasn't feeling well and I had put him to sleep. It was her first call to us, to Calvin, in nearly four months, and I did not want her to get the idea that Calvin would just be here, at the other end of the phone, whenever she felt like calling.

"I'm at my parents' place in Dallas," she said. "I'm leaving for New York in the morning, but only for a couple days on my way to Bali for three weeks."

"That sounds nice."

"Yeah. Hey, do you think he's really asleep? I mean, maybe he's still up or something. I'd really like to talk to him."

"No, he's definitely asleep. I'm not sure what he's got, a bug or something."

"Hmm."

We were silent for a long time, ten seconds or so,

until finally Kate said, "Gordon, kids grow a lot in a year and a half, don't they?"

Her voice broke slightly on the word "half," but then she was fine. I told her that yes, children, especially at Calvin's age, do grow a lot in a year and a half.

"You think," she said and then stopped, and I heard her fumbling with the telephone receiver. "Do you think he misses me? I mean, does he ever talk about me or anything?"

I did not answer right away, because I was not really sure what she wanted to hear. No, Calvin did not speak of her, specifically. But that wasn't because he did not miss her; he just didn't know her.

"Kate, do you miss him?"

"That's a funny thing," she said, filling her lungs. "Sometimes I miss him so much it's blinding. Debilitating. I mean, I can't think of anything else—not eating, sleeping, breathing, nothing. So I write him. Jesus, I have two shoe boxes full of letters to Calvin that maybe I'll give him someday. But they're letters to an older Calvin, a grownup Calvin. I don't know how to talk to him now. What to say?" She paused. "But then, other times, it's like it doesn't matter at all that I have a son out there, living his own life, away from me. Away from his mother. That I'm just some woman he doesn't know—who he'll never know. And that's okay. There's no sense of loss, no sorrow at all. Do you know about that, Gordon? Do you ever feel like that?"

"No," I said, looking out the kitchen window at Calvin as he took a mighty, loopy swing at the bottom of one of Mrs. Grafton's Persian rugs. A tiny puff of dust exploded onto him and he stepped back, coughing. Mrs. Grafton leaned down and said something, but I was too far away to hear. Calvin was smiling. "No, I never feel like that."

Kate said she would try to call from New York, before Bali. She really did want to talk to Calvin, even only to hear his voice and how it sounded. I told her that would be fine and then we hung up, Kate first.

There were times, obviously, when I thought Kate would make a marvelous parent. But the same unpredictability in her character to which I was attracted also made her reckless, dangerous. Once, I remember she wrapped herself in Christmas-tree lights and stood teetering on Calvin's miniature rocking horse while reciting Rimbaud. Calvin waddled near her side, flexing his little fingers to the rhythm of the blinking lights. Green, red, and white. Then he was babbling something in his own, new voice—sounds that meant nothing to anyone but him. The only thing keeping Kate here, I recall thinking, is the extension cord. By here, though, I meant in the living room; she could easily have unplugged herself and wandered, dark, into the bedroom or kitchen.

Some nights, when I'm depressed, I hold tight to these moments. They carry me through the loneliness once Calvin has gone to sleep. My ex-wife, a woman I had loved, speaking in rhyming couplets while dressed in a suit of holiday lights. It could happen again, for me, for Calvin. It could happen with somebody else.

Joyce Ives stands with her feet together, insteps touching, the red 7s on her heels perfectly even. She takes a step, slowly, and then another, and suddenly she is in full motion, her stance spread with its weight on her front leg. The dark ball swings heavy behind her right calf, releasing as it passes her knee, hitting the slick wooden floor with a muted thump. The sound of the ball spinning down the alley resembles a low, sustained cough, like someone trying to bring up a clot of phlegm. The ball collides with three pins, pushing them back into three more and then knocking over a final three. She has left only the rear right pin standing.

"Shit," she says, walking back to the ball return and placing her hand over a circular arrangement of holes blowing out cold air. She misses the spare and then sits down at our lighted table, marking a 9 into her box.

"I haven't bowled in a while," she says. She removes her cigarette from the ashtray and takes several long drags, leaving the filtered end close to her chin.

Rob is lounging on a shiny plastic bench behind Joyce and me, drinking coffee and eating Cheez Curls. His tan work boots are untied, the laces frayed, forming humps over their stiff tongues. This is the only place Joyce would agree to meet with him.

"Listen," I say, moving my arm over the top of the chair, so that I am facing both of them. "If you two are thinking divorce, that's one thing. But it doesn't concern this whole business at Gooland's. I know I've talked to you about this, Joyce."

She nods, pressing out her cigarette.

"All I want is what's fair for everybody. This case going any further than it already has won't do anyone any good. Especially me."

"You said that before," says Joyce. "But what about *me*? What do I get out of this? Except for a dishonest, sonofabitch husband, a fucked-up car, and a whole mess of bills." She glares at Rob, her lower lip quivering slightly.

"Things would be different if you hadn't driven through Gooland's," I say. "That changed everything. I mean, you're lucky someone didn't press charges."

"Can I press charges?" asks Rob, smiling.

Joyce huffs and walks back to the alley to throw her next ball. She is the only one of us who is bowling.

"Come on, Rob. You've gotta think about what can be done to try and clean this up. I mean, somehow the front of Gooland's has to get paid for. And we've both gotta find a way to call off Joyce."

Rob wipes bright orange Cheez Curl powder off his face, using the arm of his shirt.

"Are the two of you thinking divorce?"

Joyce rolls a strike.

"Mr. Nash, I'm not thinking about getting a divorce. Not yet."

"Well, I sure am," says Joyce, drawing a large X on her paper. "What else am I supposed to think? Goddam you, Rob." She turns to face him. "Were you just going to keep on fuckin' her, hoping I'd never find out? Doesn't six years of marriage mean squat to you?" Joyce picks up the ball again, her sweaty palms sticking against its even marbled surface. "What about now? You're no different. Living in her apartment on Labells Street. I know. You think I don't hear things, but I know."

"I'm not staying with her anymore," says Rob softly

into his shoulder. "I'm over at Kurt's place. Sleeping on his couch."

Joyce shrugs, but as she moves up the alley the corner of her mouth lifts and I can see she is pleased. Pleased that Rob is no longer living with his waitress. As she starts her motion, she murmurs under her breath, and it sounds to me like she said, "That's something, anyway."

Later, the three of us are standing at the counter waiting for a high-school-age boy to ring up Joyce's bill. She is in her stocking feet, the rental shoes resting on the glass tabletop. It costs $2.85 and Rob sets down three singles.

"I've got money," Joyce says, although she does not reach for it.

"I know. I know you do."

In the parking lot, Joyce sits on the hood of Rob's Camaro, slipping on her sneakers. Rob unlocks her car, which he is driving, and climbs in, leaving the door open while he starts it.

"You probably don't have to lock it," she says, chuckling. "I don't think there's anything to worry about."

Rob shrugs and then slams closed the door, flipping his fingers in a small wave before backing out. She nods and then looks at me, saying she has to meet a friend for dinner, but she will call me in a day or so.

Carl Miller says he has a great admiration for my father and that is why he suggested me for the job. He figured something must have rubbed off. Carl Miller is

Tarent High's basketball coach. He is lying on a narrow wooden plank positioned over the left side of his bed, his head pushed forward with pillows.

"It's a herniated disk," he says, placing his thumb against his lower back. "They're not sure if I'm going to need surgery or not."

I nod, taking a saucer and teacup from Carl's wife, Dora. I had never met the Millers before this evening, but there was a message from Harper telling me to come here, that Carl had some business to discuss.

"They want me to stay in bed for a month, see how it goes. A month, can you beat that?"

"That's a long time," I say.

Dora smiles, lowering a plate of butter cookies.

"You're not kidding." Carl reaches back and folds over the top pillow for height, so he can see me more directly. I'm sitting at the foot of his bed on a collapsible card chair.

"They think maybe, God willing, I'll be up and around sometime after Thanksgiving."

Carl wants me to fill in for him, to coach Tarent High's basketball team until he recovers.

"Harper tells me you played?"

"I wasn't very good," I say. "For three years I mostly sat on the bench at a small college back East. I also played some intramural ball in law school. But I hardly think either of those things qualifies me for a position as head coach. Really, Mr. Miller, I think there must be better-suited candidates out there. Don't you have an assistant?"

"Well"—he clasps his hands over his belt buckle—

"I did have one, but he moved. Down to Key West in June to help his brother out with a charter fishing business. Didn't know jack about fishing, but said his brother would help him with that—teach him everything he needed."

The telephone rings and Mrs. Miller gets up and points to the open doorway, as if to say she'll answer it in the other room. She leaves and after two more rings it stops and we can hear the muffled up and down tone of her voice through the wall.

"Harper also told me you did some coaching. A women's team?"

"I wouldn't exactly call that coaching. It was more like damage control. I helped out with my ex-wife's sorority team. Again, it's not something I would put on a résumé."

"Mr. Nash, how well do you know Tarent?"

I shrug and lean back in my chair. "We've been here for close to a year now. I guess I know it pretty well. It's a small town."

"Right. It's a small town. You've been down at the high school, you know what the basketball games are like. Sure, people want to see 'em win—but mostly, folks want to have fun. To have a hot dog or two, a soda, and maybe see their boy or their neighbor's boy score a few points—"

"That's another thing," I say. "I've got a son of my own. I'm at work all day and I need to be with him in the afternoons and evenings. It's just the two of us."

"You can bring him to practice and to the games.

He'd have a great time. And the boys will love him. They're good kids, Mr. Nash."

Carl Miller goes on about the character of his players and I pretend to listen, nodding occasionally while trying to make out what Mrs. Miller is talking about in the adjoining room. When he finishes, I thank him for the offer and tell him I'll give it some thought but, truly, I think he should continue looking. I fail to mention, however, that near the end of my father's life I had formed an emotional wall; I had written him off as simply nothing more than the man who provided my mother with the sperm that helped to create me. A lucky tumbler in the hay. That and a basketball coach. At this moment, the thought of following in his footsteps—in any form—leaves me nauseated, suffocated by the irony. Grief of men who were here before us, of men like my father, furnishes the diagrams to our own lives.

To be sure, I have no genuine explanation of why I have become the type of man I am today, the type of father I am with Calvin. There are times, however, when my mind drifts and I become acutely aware of the fact that I'm overcompensating. Perhaps it's because my own father failed to show much emotion toward me that I so openly heap affection on Calvin. Already, as a small boy, he is often permitted to stay awake past his bedtime or dig messy holes in the yard simply because he wants to see them flood with rainwater. Part of his little life is filled with wonder and silver sparklers and as much love as one parent can provide. He will not always have such freedom, though, because the world is not so generous.

Gripping the banister, I wave to Mrs. Miller on my way out and she smiles, mouthing the words "Nice meeting you." In the kitchen, a tin of butter cookies sits open on the table and I take a few before leaving. I tell myself they are for Calvin, but I know I'll eat them on the car ride home.

At a stop sign, my mind tumbles to a day when Kate and I were still in school. We had taken a break from our studies to shoot baskets on the asphalt court behind one of the dorms. While playing, she began to cover me tight on defense; she used her hands to check me, along the hips; she positioned herself for rebounds with her butt. She was not frantic, crazed, like some women who haven't participated in many team sports. Her footwork was also advanced, like someone who had been playing the game all her life (though she had not). And she was competitive, more competitive than me: keeping score aloud, announcing it after every bucket. Sometimes when I was squaring my body to shoot, she would yell obscenities into my ear in the hopes it would distract me.

Later that afternoon, I was again mesmerized by her footwork. This time it came as she sidestepped a lunatic ranting near the student union, his forehead bloodied, his cheeks spotted with dirt. He was wielding a deformed six-iron, buckled slightly along the end of the shaft. He swang furiously, close. Kate grabbed my hand and yanked me to her side. Then, without stopping, she said, "Keep your head down, man. You're developing a wicked hook."

Nothing will take this woman by surprise, I said to myself, even nearly getting clocked by a golf-club-brandishing nut. And now, much later, she would not be fazed upon learning that someone—some *school*—wants her ex-husband to coach its basketball team. The same guy whose most insightful advice to her sorority sisters was "Wear two pairs of athletic socks during games."

Near sundown, the house is dark except for a subdued, low-watt light coming from atop the staircase, coming from inside the bathroom. I have sent Mrs. Grafton home and have called out to Calvin several times, but he hasn't answered. Making my way upstairs, deliberately, I can hear short, high-pitched grunts followed by the whiny intake of breath. The noises sound caustic, banking off the porcelain and tile. As I reach the fourth step from the top, my eyeline becomes even with the bathroom and I can see Calvin's lower torso sprouting from within the toilet. His legs are awkwardly flailing, kicking out, the toes of his sneakers trying desperately to grab onto something. The rug has been flipped back against itself and both the trash pail and the hamper have been knocked over, spilling wads of Kleenex, disposable razors, used Q-Tips, and dirty underwear across the floor. Standing at the door, I watch as the toilet seat bangs softly down on Calvin. His left hand is submerged in toilet water and he is pushing the seat back up with his right hand, only to have it clunk down again, striking his shoulder and neck.

"Calvin," I say, placing my briefcase on the counter beside the sink, "what the *hell* are you doing?"

His response is inaudible, deep-bellied groans followed by a throaty cry.

"All right, all right. Settle down. Are you stuck?"

He nods and tries to turn and face me. His cheeks are red, damp, and swollen, mostly from rubbing against the lower toilet seat.

Sliding in close, I straddle him with my legs and slip my hand down his arm, following its smooth, puffy surface into the water. My fingers feel for his hand, which is folded tight around his thumb and jammed into the flushing hole at the bottom of the bowl. Pushing his thumb by its second knuckle, into his palm, I give a quick, sharp tug and pull him free.

Calvin climbs onto my lap and hugs me hard, crying into my necktie. Stroking his wrinkled left hand, I tell him not to worry, that he is fine. After another few minutes he stops, as if on command, and climbs to the floor. He steps back, nursing his injured paw, and kicks me in the shin.

"Hey, what was that for?"

"You took my manna-war. You threw it down the toilet."

I stand up, smiling. "Is that what you were doing? Looking for your man-o-war?"

"Yeah," he says, kicking me again. "I want it back."

"You're going to get something, all right, if you don't stop kicking me."

"Get it, Dad!" he says, stomping his foot at the base

of the toilet, which causes the seat to slap down and startle him.

"Listen, Cal," I say, mopping up the spilled water with a bath towel. "I talked to you about that man-o-war, I told you it was rotten. We saved it for as long as we could, but it got too smelly. There was nothing else I could do."

"You coulda got some more of that stuff at the doctor's. That would've made it better."

"Calvin, no it wouldn't. It had already gone bad." I hang the damp towel over the shower rod and then pick up the clothes and trash from the floor. "It was a mistake for Grandma to have sent it in the first place."

"No, it wasn't a mistake," Calvin says, running to his room. "It wasn't a mistake. It wasn't a mistake."

He has just been swimming in a toilet teeming with bacteria, and all my powers of persuasion will not get him to take a bath. Not now. Not after what's happened. I cannot even convince him to clean his little body of filmy germs.

Turning off the bathroom light, I sit down on the top step, hugging my knees close to my chest. Calvin is crying in his bedroom. And I am alone. It starts slowly, a single tear welling against my right eye before cresting over the bottom eyelid, clinging briefly to the lower lashes and then dropping, slithering down my cheek, following the straight curve of my jawline, and finally falling free, absorbed into blue pinpoint oxford cloth. Soon, it comes hard. I lie back, covering my face with the crook of my arm. My chest lifts, quivering heavy with sobs. And I am loud and I cannot stop. Rolling onto one side, I curl into a large, bent letter G. The wetness sinks into my collar, holding it flush against the skin of my neck. I try to think about why I am crying, but I do not know. Not really. Whether it is for Calvin or for myself. For my own life.

After some time, breathing comes easier. My saliva is thick and syrupy and I bring it together on the back of my tongue before swallowing hard, forcing the mucus down with the muscles of my throat. The carpet is matted, twisting into flat, stubby bunches pressed in various directions that I can feel against my forearms. In the darkness I am still, and prudently, quietly, I can sense Calvin at my side. He is standing at my left, confused by his father's tears. It is the first time he has seen me cry. Or at least the first time that he can remember.

"I'm all right," I say, sliding again onto my back.

"I'm sorry that I made you sad," he says.

I do not answer him for a moment or so. When I do, I sit up and reach for his hands, taking them into my own and holding them below my chin.

"Sweetheart, it wasn't you. *Really*. It's just a bad day. It's just—" I pause, rubbing his tiny, pink thumb against my lower lip. "It's just that I haven't done this before. Being a dad is hard and I'm not sure I'm doing it right."

He pulls his hands away and begins petting the back of my head, where the hairline turns to flesh. "You're doing good."

"I'm glad one of us thinks so."

"I think so."

I smile and kiss him on both cheeks. "I'm sorry I had to throw out your man-o-war."

He shrugs and then looks down at the toes of his sneakers. "Me too."

Indeed, being a father is difficult and there are no blueprints to insure that we do not stray, do not wander, misdirecting our children down a barbed, prickly path that they will hate us for, deeply, truly, for the rest of their cursed lives. And forgiveness is foreign. Years after I had left home, while I was in Ann Arbor, Kate asked me why I didn't talk to my father more? Why didn't I ask to speak to him after talking with my mother? Why didn't my mother insist, reaching over on their couch and putting the telephone in his hand. I told her I didn't know; we were just like that. We had never said much to each other, even during the seventeen years we lived under the same roof. Then Kate asked how about when I was a child, when my father was young?

There is not much I remember of the time I was very little, I said. And my father was never young, at least not while I was alive. I was born when my father was forty-two, and even my earliest memories of him—reed-thin, his skin red and warm, not the gray hue it would achieve in his later years; white weeds of hair pushing back above his temples, and his hands, the hands he would pass on to me, large and webbed with blue veins—even those first memories are of a man isolated from his family. Of my mother and me eating casserole or cold chicken by ourselves in the dim light of the kitchen and then her taking me to bed, sitting over me, brushing the wisps of hair from my face and telling me about the time she found me in the storage closet wearing her waxy underwear like a hat, or kneeling on a table, lapping water from my aunt's fish tank. Later, after my mother had already dressed for bed and then had fallen asleep reading a magazine or watching television, my father would come home. Most of the time he had already had his dinner, so he would sit in the dark at the kitchen table eating butter-pecan ice cream from the container and drinking beer. Often, my mother awakened and went in to ask if she could fix him eggs or a sandwich, but he would just say no, the ice cream was fine. Only once, when I was seven and sick with pneumonia, did he come in to say good night to me. Even then, he stood silently at the doorway, letting the hall light creep in cautiously with the push of his wrist, falling in a narrow block against my face. He was silent for a long time, thinking I was asleep, and then, before turning to leave, he blew me a kiss. I had opened my eyes, briefly, and I remember how awkward and uncomfortable my father looked, blowing a kiss to his only son, as if the act was completely foreign to him. And it was.

I don't ever want things to be like that between Calvin and me. But I wonder if my father had the same noble intentions when I was born, only somehow he lost his way. It wasn't necessarily that things became more important to him than his son, only that he always figured there would be time, time enough to make it up. And, of course, there never is. Mostly, I try not to hold this spacious void of emotion against my father. It is how things happened. But I don't ever want them to *happen* like that for Calvin and me. It is a large part of the reason why, after Kate left, I accepted Harper's job offer and moved to Tarent. Because I knew I would be able to spend time with Cal. To watch him eat a powdered-sugar doughnut for the first time and get it on his nose and cheeks, to have him ask me why dogs can't talk or if fish sleep, to yell at him for chasing a ball into the street, to kiss him on the lips as long as he will allow.

Now, lifting Calvin's shirt, I press my mouth hard against his belly and blow, turning slightly from side to side so it makes a loud, wet noise, like a fart. Calvin laughs and tries to push me away, but I hold him tight from behind, spraying spit onto his chest until he has had enough.

FIVE

The floorboards are tanned and brittle, creaky beneath their slick varnished glaze. At the center is an enormous crimson circle with a gray letter T painted in its middle, barely touching the inside of the circle's edges. Tired black girders drop from the ceiling, holding Plexiglas backboards above both ends of the floor. Two baskets, evenly spaced, set along each side of the court, can be raised or lowered depending on need. Near the main doorway, below three large dangling heaters, is a pair of long wooden grandstands that pull out for seating. High on the far wall is a scoreboard protected by thin wire fencing, with Trojans listed on one side and Visitors on the other.

There is another set of grandstands across from the first, and these have been opened, revealing six levels, the lowest only two feet or so behind a white line that encompasses the floor. The room's light is a warm orange, soothing, not harsh like the bold neon that is used in most of the newer gymnasiums. A few boys dressed in shorts, T-shirts, and high-top sneakers lie stretched out on the open grandstand, talking. Several others are shooting basketballs into two of the far baskets, but instead of chasing after their missed shots, they simply reach into a large, wheeled hamper and pull out another ball. Calvin seems to like the idea of a limitless supply of balls and he lets go of my hand and runs over to where the boys are shooting.

"Come here, Cal. Before you hurt yourself," I say.

A stocky boy with a crew cut bends down beside Calvin, holding a basketball out in front of himself, carefully, like a melon.

"You play, fella?" he asks, pulling the ball away as Calvin reaches for it.

Calvin moans, missing as he swipes for the ball, instead grabbing a narrow band of cloth from the boy's tank top and yanking it off the boy's shoulder.

"Hey, Calvin. That's enough," I say, turning toward the boy. "I'm Gordon Nash. I think Coach Miller mentioned that I might be filling in for him."

"Oh, yeah. Sure." The boy stands, dropping the basketball back into the hamper. "He called us last night."

"This is my son, Calvin."

"I'm Peter Sawyer."

He shakes my hand and then tries to do the same with Calvin, but Calvin wants no part of it and he hides his face behind my thigh.

"He's shy, huh?" asks Peter Sawyer, tucking his tank top down into his shorts.

"Sometimes," I say, reaching back and leading Calvin around to the front of my legs. "And sometimes he just wants attention."

The rest of the boys gather by Peter Sawyer and I introduce Calvin and myself. There are eleven of them, and two absent. They move back to the open grandstand and sit scattered, sneakers untied and socks rolled down tight to their ankles, in the style of the day.

"I have never really coached before," I say, seating Calvin at the end of the first row and setting my briefcase down beside him. "I will try to do my best. Obviously, I don't know any of you and I don't know your abilities. So, as far as I'm concerned, you're all the same—starting at ground zero."

Most of them are staring at points off behind me, with shallow expressions on their faces. Except for Calvin, who truly appears interested, for he has never heard me talk this way, and certainly never to a captive audience this size. His head is cocked and his mouth forms a supple, pink O.

"I suppose," I say, and then fall silent. Although it has not turned especially cold yet, one of the space heaters over my shoulder clicks on, rattling with a tinny belch at first and then settling into a steady, low-pitched hum. "Really, I'm not a basketball coach at all. I'm a father—a lawyer." The decision came to me several nights ago, as I lay nearly asleep in the gentle darkness of my bedroom: if I made an effort, I could manage coaching this team for a few months. I would not allow those fears of mirroring my father, of being like him in ways I could not tolerate, to stop me from attempting something I might actually enjoy—that Calvin might enjoy, too. Perhaps, along with the delicate attention to the details of daily life, basketball might serve to bring Calvin and me closer together, which is exactly what it did not do for my own father and me. "Mostly, I'm just trying to help out Coach Miller."

Peter Sawyer smiles when I look his way and then drops his eyes, hypnotized by the dark cuticle pattern in the wooden seat beneath him.

"Let's . . . let's make this fun. All right?"

Most of the boys nod. At first, I have them run a simple lay-up drill, forming two lines, one at each side of the basket. After a while, they switch sides, shooting instead from the left. Then I call out Peter Sawyer and another boy and have them choose teams for a scrimmage, with each boy introducing himself to me after he is picked. Midway through the selection process, one of the missing boys walks in, barefoot, his sneakers tied together, slung over his right shoulder.

"Hey, wait a minute," says Peter, gesturing toward the new boy and then turning to me. "He'd have been my first or second pick. Now they've got Eric *and* Noah. They're the two best players."

Eric Shaw, the first selection, is nearly six feet six inches tall—lean, with sharp, well-defined muscles stretched tight over his bones, creating thin, mottled ridges that catch crescents of light on his tobacco-colored skin. His calves are narrow as forearms and he walks on the balls of his feet with a quick, short bounce. His hair is shorn close as a shadow, leaving only stubble.

The late arrival is Noah Ward. He sits on the floor, bunching his socks before slipping them on his chalky feet. I recognize him as one of the letter-jacket-clad boys from the football game Calvin and I attended a month or so ago. Noah was the boy driving the pickup truck with the miniature basketball sneakers swinging from the rearview mirror. His face is narrow and angular, with a minor constellation of freckles spattered across the bridge of his nose. Bisecting the nearly perfect oval of his left earlobe is a small, gold hoop earring. He doesn't seem concerned in the least which team he ends up on, or that he has interrupted practice.

"Why're you late?" I ask.

"Just one of those unavoidable things, you know?"

"No, I don't know. I believe this is what's called getting off to a bad start. So let's try again. Why are you late?"

"Girl problems," he answers, rising to his feet.

Someone mutters something under his breath about a person named Ann and a few of the other boys snicker.

"Look, y'all don't have to be here if you've got better things to do with your time," I say, preparing to kick a basketball from out of my path. But I stop, realizing I sound an awful lot like my father when he was coaching. These are boys, simply boys, and this is a game. It should be fun. Which is something my father, in his later years, simply forgot. "I didn't really mean that. Well, I did, but not in that tone. Nobody has to be here if they don't want. Really. But if you do, let's try and accord each other a little respect. If someone has trouble at home, or with school or a girl," I say, glancing at Noah, "then I'd be glad to talk to him about it. I know I'm new and you don't know me from Adam, but I'm a pretty good listener. Christ, it hasn't been all that long since I was in high school. Right, Cal?" Calvin is steering the hamper of balls around in circles, but he pretends to know what I am talking about and he answers with a nod. "Otherwise, let's try and get here on time."

They play forty minutes of basketball, enough for me to get a rough idea of how much talent each boy has. Eric Shaw is spectacular, clearly the best, with Noah Ward and a boy named Russell Johns next. After the scrimmage, they distribute a few balls and tell me they have to punch out—which means make one final long-range shot before exiting the gym. They scurry, chasing down missed baskets nearly as fast as they hoist them. In several minutes, only Cy Connell is left. He is painfully thin, with a slight curve to his posture raising unavoidably between his shoulder blades. A gray pallor about his cheeks and neck makes the dark, half-moon-shaped wells below his eyes appear almost black. When shooting, he lowers the ball close to his chest, like Calvin, so as to get all his weight behind each effort. If he did this in a game, the ball would be blocked before it rose above his forehead. Most of his shots do not even strike the rim or backboard, and after a few more, he turns to see if I am still watching.

"You'll be here all night," says Noah, heading off to the locker room.

I move to where Cy is standing, placing my hands on his triceps.

"First, you've got to try and shoot from here," I say, pushing his arms up so his elbows are level with his shoulders. "It'll take some getting used to. And walk in a few steps. There's no reason for you to be this far back."

"You're not supposed to punch out from close."

"Who says?"

"I'm not sure," he answers. "It's just the way everyone else does it."

"Maybe you're not everyone else."

When he shoots above his face, as I've shown him, the ball twists off to the left, dropping even shorter of its goal than the old way. He tries several more and I tell him it looks better, although I am lying.

Crunched against the far wall, his knees near his ears, Calvin watches, puckering his lips as if he swallowed something sour. For a brief moment, in the refracted school-hall light, he resembles his mother, this image I have of her not long after we discovered she was pregnant. She was resting on the stairs to our apartment building, late-afternoon sunshine banking off the picture window above her shoulders, as she sucked the pink and purple and blue sand from a bag of Pixy Stix. Later, in the darkness of our bedroom, I awakened and walked to the kitchen for a glass of tap water. When I returned to our bed, I recall wishing it could always be like that afternoon: Kate waiting for me at home, alone, her hair tied back loosely with a cotton band, her mouth powdered with granules of sweet, colored sugar. Pregnant. We could hold our lives like a spool of twine, letting it unravel at whatever speed we chose. Then, watching the bed, her chest slowly sinking and climbing, I had a series of horrible thoughts, appalling premonitions that I would force an accident with a delicate shove or errant elbow —bony, direct. An accident that might cause the fetus to abort. Leak down Kate's thighs in soupy yokes of blood—tissue as delicate and transparent as rice paper.

Eventually, the feelings subsided. There were other times, though, in the ensuing months when those same thoughts would rise again like a watery blister, hateful and hot.

The first thing Calvin does when we get home is to take our basketball out and try to dribble it across the porch. Of course, he is unable to, and after a few pats the ball rolls away from him, bounceless. He chases after it, again lifting the ball chest-high and then releasing it, slapping it with both palms. This time, the ball caroms off his foot and down the stairs.

"What're you doing?" I ask.

"I'm just gonna play a little."

"No, you're not. You told me you were hungry."

"That was before."

"Before what?"

He pauses, looking puzzled, and then says, "Just before."

"Calvin, it's too dark to play now. Besides, if you don't eat soon you're going to get a Belly Cat."

When Calvin was younger and got hunger pangs, Kate would place her ear to his stomach and say, "Hey, do you hear that growling? I know what your problem is, you've got a cat in there. A Belly Cat."

"I don't have Billy Cat," he says, descending the stairs, his hand at nose level, gripping the rail. "I had him before."

"See, that's worse. He's gone hiding and now he's gonna come back even meaner."

"Uh-uh."

"Sure is. So come on and let's get something in there."

After dinner, Calvin and I sit in a hammock that is strung from column to column on the side of the porch. We are eating brownies that Mrs. Grafton baked and left on a cellophane-covered plate in our kitchen. The two of us swing back and forth, my feet grounded, Calvin's barely hanging over the edge, toes pointed inward. When I kick us higher, he turns to me and says "Whoa," flashing teeth coated in fudgy mortar.

"Did you like that today?" I ask.

He nods and then takes another bite of brownie.

"Do you think you'd like to do it for a while?"

He shrugs. "Everday?" he manages, brown spittle flecking his chest.

"Maybe not every day. I mean, some days you'd go over to Meg's house, and other days you'd stay with Mrs. Grafton."

"I like all the balls."

"Yeah, I know you do. You never saw that many in one place, huh?"

He shakes his head. Sitting up, he tries to climb off, but his hand slips through the rope webbing.

"Where are you going?"

"I wanna get another brownie, before I lose my ap'tite."

I lift him across my lap, holding his dirty hands close

to his belt buckle, so they won't wipe off on anything else.

"Hang on a second. I want to talk to you about something. Do you know what I was doing today?"

"Uh-uh."

"I was coaching basketball—or at least trying."

"Are you gonna still have your office?"

"Oh, sure. I'm just doing this to help out."

"Help who?"

"To help Mr. Miller, the regular basketball coach. To help the school. And to help the kids, I suppose."

"I liked the kids."

I smile and brush brownie from his chin. "They liked you, too." At times, it is difficult to know exactly what to say to a little boy, what he's equipped to understand.

Calvin knots up the corner of his mouth and shrugs.

"You know what I was just telling you, about coaching basketball? About being a basketball coach? Well, that's what my own father used to do. That was his job."

"He's from Kansas?"

"No, he wasn't from Kansas. He coached at a school in Ohio. You once visited him there when you were a baby."

"A long time ago."

"Not so long," I say, loosening my grip on his hands. "About four years." I lower Calvin to the ground and tell him to be careful not to tip the plate over and spill the brownies. I also tell him to take only one.

When he returns, he sits on the chafed wooden floorboards in front of me, his legs pressed flat.

"You didn't bring me any?" I ask, furrowing my eyebrows and pretending to look angry. But Calvin is not fooled. He has seen this act before. "No milk, either?"

"It's too high."

"Too high, huh? How come I've seen you pull a chair over to get cookies down from the cupboard, but you don't do it for the milk?"

"It's 'cuz . . ." He stops, looking around for something to occupy my attention, to take my mind off the question. "Well, 'cuz the floor is slippery by the milk and I don't wanna fall."

"That's good," I say. "But I don't think you should chance it anywhere in there, okay? No more standing on chairs to get things down."

He drops his head, stuffing the last corner of brownie into his mouth.

"Hey, Cal. Do we understand each other here?"

Reluctantly, he nods and lets out a brownie-muffled "Uh-huh." And then, "Did I see all the balls in Ohio?"

It is a peculiar question, but I know exactly what he's talking about. "I'm not sure. I know they were there—more even. But you were so tiny that I'm not sure we brought you into the gym. We didn't want you to get hurt."

"Oh."

Everything is still, so quiet that I can hear the din of the refrigerator through the screen door. Calvin lies back and begins to make mock snow angels against the wood. "I bet I did see the balls," he says. And then he stops.

SIX

It is simply another small piece of my life, I tell myself, thinking now of these newfound duties as basketball coach. It's just a piece whose shape I'm not sure of yet. Sitting in the cramped, boxy office of Tarent High's physical-education staff, I wipe the sweat from my face and the back of my neck, using a nubby orange towel. Noah Ward is standing akimbo in the doorway, eagerly shifting his weight from one leg to the other. He wants his earring, which I made him remove during practice and surrender to me. It was his third warning, and as I explained to him earlier, I am not opposed to ear wear on men, I just don't want it getting caught on someone else's shirt and ripping open his earlobe. Today, it is a petite diamond stud and I take it from my breast pocket and flip it to him.

"The backing's gone," he says.

"What?"

He holds the earring up to the light, turning it by

the face so that I can only see the slender gold stem sticking out.

"See, the back part's missing. That's what holds it onto my ear."

Pressing my shirt breast flat, I can feel the tiny backing clinging to the stitching at the bottom of my pocket. I dangle two fingers down and retrieve it, handing Noah the butterfly-shaped piece of metal.

"Thanks," he says, sarcastically, and then turns to leave.

"Hey!"

Noah stops in the hallway, but does not look back.

"In case you hadn't noticed, you're starting to piss me off. I won't cut anybody from this team for not being good enough. But I will cut someone for being an asshole."

As he leaves, the bulb in the table lamp flickers and then, with a wispy pop, burns out. I sit in the dark, my hands spread out like enormous spiders over my kneecaps.

"What do you think about someone who won't listen?" I ask aloud, to myself. In a moment, the words are gone, as swiftly and trail-less as they came. Like something my father would have said, maybe to one of his own players or maybe to me, not really expecting an answer.

More than he needs basketball or permissive girlfriends or diamond earrings, big ones, this boy, Noah, wants to leave Tarent; he wants to abandon his family and Kansas and the Middle West. In ways, some ways, he is like me at that age. Nothing in his life, now, will fit. It is time to move on, to find other people with whom to connect. Twice, when I was young, I ran away from home—once for six hours and another time for almost three days. It is difficult for those around you to know, exactly, how to repair what, to them, doesn't seem broken. For Noah, and perhaps Calvin one day, I jab blindly at commonalities: something that will not cause him to cringe, something that will not create distance. But maybe, with Noah, I'm just not so good. Finally, ultimately, I don't understand—as my father didn't understand with me.

Carl Miller has left half a pack of cigarettes in his desk drawer and I feel around for matches. The cigarettes are unfiltered and they burn my lungs as I take a draw. Someone has turned out the light in the hallway, leaving only the tack-sized glow of the cigarette to break the darkness. Holding to an independent, bottomless timbre, I can hear the boys' voices echo from within the showers. There is a leathery slapping sound and then a loud voice warns everyone to watch out for flying soap. In six days we will play our first game, against nearby Carbon Springs, and I wonder how a coach is supposed to know when (and if) his team is ready. Certainly, it will become apparent after the game begins. But what about before then? Although I have told them on several occasions that it really doesn't matter to me whether or not we win, I am not sure they believe it. We underestimate the minds of youth, fresh and steady as rain.

The end of the cigarette has grown soggy with saliva, sticking to a crease in my lower lip. Yesterday Calvin received a postcard from Kate, who is still in Bali, but I haven't read it to him yet. I will wait. The postcard depicts a green lizard flicking its shiny tongue, with the words *Greetings from Bali* written in light gray cursive across the top. She apologizes (to both of us) for not calling before she left, but says she had last-minute trouble with her passport. She tells Calvin that there are lizards and chameleons everywhere and people have to look down when they walk so they won't step on them. Calvin will love this, she imagines. He will ask me if we can go there, too. And if I were a father with money, lots of it, I would take him and let him collect as many lizards and chameleons as his spindly arms could carry.

There is so much I don't know; so many things are not easy. Often, I wonder how this life found me. What I had wanted was to be a trial attorney, a litigator. To practice law, really *practice* it. Perform in courtrooms with slippery maple banisters and marble walkways and people, lots of people, weighted down with documents and urgency. And to live someplace with contemporary art galleries and Thai restaurants and public transportation. Someplace un-Kansas.

But here I am, settling a homestead on the grainy, wind-burned soil of the Great Plains. And last week I sat out behind our porch, cutting hemp rope into sections for a winter storm fence and wrapping the ends with twine so it wouldn't unravel. Whipping is what they call it—whipping the end of a rope.

Who is there to talk to about such things? The "fellas" at Duritz Hardware? Afterwards, the rope bound and stored like garden hose, I walked into the kitchen, swollen with the fuzzy pride of accomplishment. Look what I did, I wanted to announce to someone with whom I could share a six-pack. Instead, I found Calvin rocking his knuckles against the refrigerator, leaving fine dimples of blackberry jam. He appeared bewildered, listening to the scraping sound of the seeds against the smooth door. Troubled. Like a little fucking retard-boy. He knew his actions were wrong. My anger came quick, prickling along the elastic skin of my throat. I grabbed the first thing I could, whatever was close. Chewing half a paper napkin, I blew spit wads at Calvin—small, white amoebas that filled his face like sores.

Later, I closed the door to my room and pressed my lower back against the bottom—sort of a human doorjamb. Calvin stayed in the hall, gurgling, kicking. Sometimes—many times—I simply want to be alone. Son-less and alone. Let me figure this life out by myself.

Now the office smells of cigarette smoke. There is something soothing, almost cathartic about sitting in the dark. Like you belong among the desks and chairs and bookshelves; you are no longer simply surrounded by objects, but you become part of them. Even if someone else were to enter the room, you would remain hidden, a piece of living, breathing furniture to be passed over with a flashlight.

Shortly after Calvin and I first moved to Tarent, the two of us were sitting Indian-style on the floor of what is now Calvin's bedroom—me refolding clothes that had been disturbed along the trip, and Calvin watching, rolling a toy race car back and forth over his shin. Suddenly, one of the town's generators stopped working, although we didn't know this at the time, and the electricity in our house shut off. The two of us were quiet for a few moments and then, very matter-of-factly, Calvin said, "So this is Kansas." I thought it a very profound statement for someone his age and I told him so, though he did not understand. And later, when I leaned over him at bedside, a candle flickering brick-colored hues onto his face, he asked if it would always be this way, without lights. I said no, that they would be up again in the morning. "We need them more at night," he said, blowing the candle so hard that the milky wax pooled around the wick jumped, splattering his night table with flecks that hardened before I left the room.

A loud smacking noise breaks my train of thought —the thumping as a ball is kicked into the hallway walls, followed by Charlotte's voice telling Calvin to come back and hold her hand because she cannot see anything.

"There's a row of light switches right outside the door," I say, rising and stepping into the hall.

"Oh, good," Charlotte says, with a start. "That's better."

Briefly, Calvin has disappeared. But as I prepare to yell for him, he rounds the corner, his shirt half-untucked, banded with a large stripe of black grease rising nearly to his chest.

"What happened to you?" I ask.

"Nuthin'."

"What do you mean, '*nuthin'*'? How did that get on your shirt?"

"From underneath."

"Underneath what?"

"That," he says, pointing at an enormous steel dolly used to roll wrestling mats into the gymnasium. "I was tryin' to get the ball out."

"How'd the ball get there in the first place?"

Calvin shrugs.

"Did you kick it there?"

"Maybe. I'm not really sure. See, I kicked it first . . . and then . . . well—"

"Okay. Sit down in there"—I gesture toward Coach Miller's office—"and we'll try to clean."

After I have wiped as much of the grease from Calvin's shirt as will come off without the aid of a washing machine, we say our goodbyes to Charlotte and leave for the supermarket. Once there, we don't take long to fill our cart, for now we have the routine down to a science. The science of a single father and his son buying only those things that they truly need to survive the week: milk, skinless chicken parts, bottled tomato sauce, elbow-shaped pasta, cans of soup, baked beans, and corn, apples, bananas to be sliced onto cereal. Then the trade-off: the son grimacing as the father takes iceberg lettuce, celery stalks, mushrooms, and fresh green beans; the son pointing to animal-shaped cookies, ice cream, and, not to forget, chocolate-flavored sauce. The total is not expensive, for in Tarent, Kansas, it does not cost much to feed one and a half people.

We sit in the parking lot behind the Stop 'n' Shop, Calvin holding the can of chocolate sauce against his thigh, for fear of losing it among the six bags lining the backseat. Suddenly, a small brown pebble-shaped object lands on the hood of the car with a ping. Then, slowly, another and another, until finally, in a rush, an avalanche of the objects slams down in a heap with such force that it causes the car to sway slightly forward. It also causes Calvin to jerk back, as if a victim of whiplash, and scream out in terror. The car is parked in a slot directly beside an eight-foot-high ramp leading into the back of the store, and as I get out, I can see a woman leaning over the rail, still clinging to a once-swollen green-and-red bag.

"Oh, gosh," she says, smoothing out the bag against her stomach and chest. "I'm *so* sorry. I kinda lost my grip and as it slipped I tried to catch it on the railing, but it split open at the bottom."

She is talking about the bag, which, as it turns out, was filled with Purina Dog Chow.

"You want to feed your dog from the hood of my car?" I ask.

She straightens, at first not sure if I am serious or not. But we both smile at the same time and then she quickly starts down the ramp, toward the front end of my car. Her hair is a light, buttery red, cut blunt above the slope of her shoulders. She is wearing a black turtleneck and oversized, faded jeans that are frayed white at the knees and back pockets. They are cinched loosely around her waist by a wide belt with an oblong, silver Western buckle.

"Look at this," she says, staring at the mound of dog food. "I'm so sorry. Really."

"Don't worry about it."

"Oh, Jesus! I've scared him to death."

She is looking through the windshield at Calvin, who is still pale and squeezing the can of syrup with both hands.

"Come on out here, Cal."

I walk over to his side of the car and unfasten his safety belt, pulling him free. But he has not removed his eyes from the pile, mesmerized by its unfamiliarity.

"It's dog food, Cal," I say, taking a kernel that managed to lodge itself under the windshield wiper and handing it to him. "See?"

He taps at it with his fingernail, and then releases a long sigh that practically forces his rib cage in upon itself. "Dog food," he says, as if he knew all along. As if that is the only possible thing it could be.

"Well," she says, cocking her head and walking a few steps closer. "I guess what we need is a giant Dustbuster."

Calvin climbs on the bumper and shoves his face toward the pile, taking several sniffs.

"How 'bout this?" I remove a box of plastic trash bags from our groceries. "We could fill a couple of these and then you can still use the food."

"Oh, wow. That would be great."

Her eyes are a slate-blue with tiny, precise pupils that seem nearly to explode when she reaches for a trash bag.

"Here you go, Cal," I say, handing him a bag, too. "Fill 'er up."

He looks puzzled, so I grab two palmfuls of dog food and dump them into his bag.

"With hands?" he asks, for I am constantly telling him not to use his hands, to use a fork or spoon or shovel instead. How can adults be trusted? he must wonder.

"Yep. With hands."

He smiles and then digs in, balancing the dog food against the insides of his wrists and forearms. As he tips the food into the bag, a few pieces drop on the asphalt lot.

"Careful. See if you can keep any from falling on the ground."

He is concentrating now, his tongue folded between his teeth and lips at the corner of his mouth. Every few seconds he turns to look at me or at the woman, as if to let us know that he's doing it right, making a contribution.

The dog food will fit into one bag, but we use three, not wanting the plastic to tear when lifted. The woman has tight, closely carved muscles and I can see those in the back of her thighs flex, pulling up the slack in her jeans as she bends over. We dump the sacks into the back of her truck, which is dark blue and dirty and familiar. Hanging from the rearview mirror are a pair of red-and-black-and-white miniature sneakers, the same sneakers that belong to Noah Ward. When I ask her if this is Noah's truck she says it is not, that it is hers but she lets him drive it most days, while she is working. She says Noah is her younger brother, and from the way she speaks of him, the tone of her voice, I get the sense I'm not the first person to have had trouble with him. She is a veterinarian-in-training, but she also tends bar three nights a week at Cale's, which is two blocks from my office. Sometimes Harper and I eat lunch there. She also tells me her name is Zoe.

Calvin has been uninterested in Zoe and my conversation and he is hoisting himself onto the truck's running board to peer into the window at a quite excited dog. Zoe walks over and opens the door, setting loose a large golden retriever who begins running around in a panic, not sure what to smell first.

"This is Argos," says Zoe, crouching down to rub the dog on its neck.

"Huh?" says Calvin.

"Argos. He's named after Ulysses' dog in the *Odyssey*. Do you know what that is?"

She looks toward me when she asks the question and I shake my head.

"Of course not." She seems slightly embarrassed. "He's named from a book. After a dog in a book."

This Calvin understands, and while he pets Argos he turns to me and asks, "Do we have that book?"

"I'm not sure, Cal. Maybe packed up with the stuff in the basement."

"Oh." He waits a moment and says, " 'Cuz I'd like to hear it."

He likes the idea that a dog's name can come from a book. Then, inspired, Calvin runs to where our car is parked and bends to pick up several pieces of spilled dog food, which he promptly surrenders to Argos.

"Cal, you have to ask people before you go feeding their dog."

Halfheartedly he turns to Zoe and says, "Can I feed Ar-gus?"

"Sure."

Zoe and I lean against the back of her truck while Argos sits patiently, eagerly, as Calvin dispenses one kernel at a time.

"So, how do you know my brother?"

"From school. I'm kind of filling in for Carl Miller coaching the basketball team."

"And do you like it?"

"Really, I don't think I'm very good. I mean, it's not like I've got any experience."

"But do you like it?"

"Yeah." I pause, because I had not really thought about that question until now. "I guess I do."

"What about the boys? How have they been treating you?"

"Oh, they're fine."

"Really?"

She is grinning and I'm not sure what she is leading at.

"Most of them."

"Ahh," she says, crossing her arms. "Just most of them. Any troublemakers you'd care to point out?"

Now I start to smile, too. "I'll take the Fifth."

"That's all right. He's a pain in the ass for us, too."

Calvin comes over and wants a few more pieces of dog food, from inside the knotted bags. I tell him no, that we need to be getting some food in him.

Argos shakes himself through the scissor of Calvin's legs, from behind, and Calvin grabs the dog's collar and begins play-riding, like on a horse.

"Give a whinny," says Zoe, looking Argos in the eyes.

"He could be my pet horse," says Calvin.

"Have you ever been on a horse?"

At first, Calvin says nothing, and then, "On a real horse?"

"Yep. On a real horse."

He shakes his head.

"Maybe sometime you'd like to go for a ride on my horse."

Calvin's mouth opens wide, with awe, as if he is going to shout out with excitement. Just as suddenly he slams it shut, tipping his head and staring at Zoe with quizzical, somewhat doubting eyes. "Do you *really* have a horse?"

"Sure I have a horse. Do you think I'd promise you a horse ride if I didn't?"

Calvin shrugs and then turns to me, tugging at the sleeve of my jacket. "Hey, maybe we could go over there now for a little ride," he says.

"Not now, Cal. Another day."

"When other day? Tomorrow? Could we go tomorrow?"

"Actually, tomorrow's not so good for me," Zoe says. "But how's Saturday?"

"How's Saturday, Pop?"

They have me cornered. I tell them Saturday afternoon is good and then Zoe writes down the directions on the back of a McDonald's napkin to where her horse is stabled. She uses a felt-tip pen and the ink bleeds sloppy.

During the car ride home, Calvin is full of questions about the horse ride: Will he have to wear boots? Will he get to ride by *himself*? How big is a real horse? Could he have his own horse someday? However, I am more interested in Zoe and I ask Calvin what he thought of her.

"I like her hair," he says. "It's like berries."

"Berries? You mean like blueberries?"

"No," he answers, laughing because he knows I'm being silly. "The other kind."

"Raaathaberries?" I ask, in my best Elmer Fudd voice.

He shakes his head and turns away, mimicking my pronunciation of the word "raspberries" several times into the seat cushion.

"Huh? Is that it?"

"No. The other, other kind. You know, with the dots on them."

"Oh, strawberries."

"Yeah, strawberries. But like the inside part—the pink part."

And he is right. Zoe's hair is like the inner layer of a strawberry before its nearly white center.

"What else did you like about her?"

He shrugs because he is not sure. He knows he likes the fact that she has a horse, and a dog named Argos. Had I pointed them out, he would also have liked the sneakers hanging from her rearview mirror. But he doesn't know what, if anything, he likes about Zoe herself. It is times like these I wish, momentarily, Calvin were older. That I could talk to him, man to man, about the intangible things that attract me to a woman and he would know what I meant. That there is something in the way she smiles, pulling her upper lip tight across the row of straight, fine teeth, turning her head slightly to the left every time. The way she unconsciously twists her ankle to the side, kicking out the heel of her boot and drawing a tiny line in the gravel with its edge while she talks. That when I got close enough, once while leaning over to grab another trash bag, I could see the clean, white down on her cheeks as it caught the light. Mostly, that I haven't had this fluttery feeling about a woman in a long, long time and I just want it to last a few days more. Until I find out she is married or moving to Wyoming or simply not interested in me, a single father and his son.

Later, after we have unpacked the groceries and eaten dinner and Calvin has gone upstairs to prepare for bed, I recall the first time I had these feelings about Kate. It was a late-summer night in Ann Arbor and I had gone to meet a couple of friends on the patio of a bar we frequented. There were a lot of people, and after fighting my way through the crowd, I stood against the front staircase and decided to wait a brief while longer before giving up and heading home. After a few minutes two women drifted to the edge of the stairs and began talking. They were loud and I was kind of half paying attention to their conversation, something about the grooming habits of an art-history professor they both had—the way his square-shaped beard flipped up at the corners, like a Viking's. Then one of them, Kate, turned to me and asked if guys thought that facial hair was a good look, if we thought most women liked it. But before I could answer, before I actually realized they were talking to me, they both started laughing, and Kate gave her friend a small shove.

"Really," said Kate, "my friend here thinks you're cute."

The friend, Bonnie Atler, socked Kate in the arm and then, with a long, throaty hiss, turned and walked away.

"Jesus," said Kate, adjusting a brown leather book bag she had slung at an angle across her shoulder, chest, and back like an archer's tube of arrows. "Well . . ."

"Well."

"This isn't how it was supposed to work out."

"How exactly was it supposed to work out?" I asked, suddenly intrigued.

"Bonnie—that's my friend—she was supposed to stay and I was supposed to leave."

"Oh."

"Yeah, oh."

The music was louder and they were playing a song I liked. Midway through, as if on command, Kate sang out one of the lines: *She calls me baby, she calls everybody baby.* Although it doesn't really mean anything, the line has always been one of my favorites, one that I might have sung myself. I can't really explain it, but at that exact moment I knew Kate and I would become close. That there was something about her I liked, and after I bought her two Budweisers and a bag of honey-roasted peanuts, I told her so. Though she wasn't sure there was anything about me she was particularly fond of, she accepted a dinner invitation for the following Thursday, and I spent that week—in fact, most of the next twenty-eight months—in a thick, sticky swoon.

Beside me, Calvin has left an unopened package of bubble gum on the end table touching our couch. He knows that he is not allowed to chew gum without my permission, and I'm glad to see him following this rule. I take a piece, blowing several large, loud bubbles before sitting down to work. The Iveses have agreed to settle out of court, to split the cost for repairs at Gooland's. Still, they aren't sure whether or not they want to end their separation. Last week, Rob moved back in with Joyce, but it only lasted two days. She was fixing him a bologna sandwich and he, absent-mindedly, asked for mayonnaise. She told him that she had been making him bologna sandwiches since before they were married, since when he was still in high school and living with his folks on Kraymar Street, and never in all those years had he ever asked for mayonnaise. Joyce said "his little waitress" must have made them that way. Then she threw the jar across the kitchen at him and it broke open against a cupboard, leaving gooey curls of mayonnaise she ignored until they turned tan and firm.

Perhaps Joyce was too analytical—just let Rob have his mayonnaise. At times, things were like that for me: it was difficult to separate the literal language of the law from common conversation, especially with Kate. The exoskeleton of attorneys still remains; I wring myself for answers, for anything that might help me understand why our relationship failed.

Since meeting Zoe, Calvin has been quiet and well behaved. After basketball practice or dinner, he will leave me alone, laying himself stomach-down on the living-room floor and coloring in his books or drawing pictures. It is a horse, he will announce suddenly, holding up a stick figure that more closely resembles a piece of furniture than a four-legged animal. Then he is quiet again. He will usually do this two or three times in an evening and finally, after the last one, he will climb on my lap and make a gift of the pictures. I will act surprised, as if he hasn't done this before, as if I cannot believe someone with my blood coursing through his meandering veins could possibly draw anything so artistic. He will laugh and then kiss me good night. There are seven horses—three blue, two purple, and two brown—scribbled onto manila paper stacked neatly on the corner of my dresser. Last night, when I was tucking Calvin into bed, he asked me what kind of sounds horses make. First I whinnied into his neck, which made him laugh. Then I made a clucking noise with my tongue against the roof of my mouth while I trotted four fingers across the hump that his knees formed underneath the blanket. Calvin was enthralled, his eyes locked to my hand as I moved it back and forth, until I lifted it into the air and made a whooshing sound, like a plane, which brought him out of his trance, shaking his head.

This I have learned: children, much like adults, will fasten on some event, no matter how small or seemingly meaningless, drifting in their futures, and allow it to carry them through the rigors of daily life. Oftentimes, they have no idea they are even doing this, as with Calvin and the horse ride. Or, if he were older and wiser, he might hypothesize the same of me with Zoe.

Russell Johns is dribbling past the half-court circle, holding two fingers up in a peace sign to signal our number 2 play. Eric Shaw slides into position, on the left wing beyond the free-throw line. He is being guarded by Noah Ward, and as good as Noah is, he is not quick enough to stay with Eric. Russell passes the ball to Eric, who pump-fakes Noah off his feet and then drives past him for an easy lay-up.

"Okay," I say, waving them to a halt. "There, you've got to keep your feet, Noah. And, Chris, you've got to come over with weak-side help. You can't allow an uncontested lay-up." I grab Chris Rayles and move him in front of Eric. Then I push Ned Morrow into position on Chris's man. "Everyone's got to be aware of what his responsibilities are—not just with his own man, but with the other guys out on the floor." I point to Pat Booth standing alone near the three-point arc. "If we play smart defense they're going to have to kick the ball back out for a longer shot. Then we rotate back into position." I roll my hand and each player walks back to his original man. "Good. Okay, foul shots."

Most days, we end practice with ten minutes or so of free-throw shooting, several players at each basket. When Calvin hears this, he climbs down from the bleachers and stands next to Peter Sawyer, his favorite player.

Peter lets Calvin rebound and chase loose balls for him. When Peter's finished shooting, he always stays to play a little longer with Calvin. Usually, he lets Calvin try to dribble or, more likely, carry the ball past him and throw it toward the rim. Before I lock up the balls, Calvin usually yells "Dunk" to Peter and Peter lifts Calvin onto his shoulders so that he can slam the ball through the hoop. It is Saturday morning and midway through the free-throw shooting Calvin comes up and asks me if it is time yet, time to go horseback riding at Zoe's farm.

"No dunking today, Cal?" Peter says.

I give Calvin a little pat and he tepidly shuffles over to Peter, allowing himself to be lifted and then, without his usual zeal, dropping the ball down through the rim. Almost immediately, he runs back to my side and tells me to hurry with the balls.

"You know who this is?" I ask Calvin as I grab Noah before he heads into the locker room.

"Kinda," he answers, shrugging.

"Who?"

"One of the team."

"Yeah, but who?"

He doesn't know and he bobs his head, sucking on the underside of his lip.

"This is Noah. He is Zoe's brother."

"Her brother?"

"Uh-huh."

Calvin steps closer to Noah, reaching out as if he is going to touch him, but then leaving his small hand in the air for a moment before dropping it back down to his side.

"Do you have a horse, too?"

"No."

"Your sister does."

Noah nods.

"She's letting me ride it today."

Noah nods again and then, almost uncomfortably, says, "It's a great horse."

"I got these boots," says Calvin, sticking out his left foot to reveal a new, tan Timberland lace-up.

"Those are cool. I used to have a pair like that."

"I used to have a manna-war but we had to throw it out. It got rotten."

A slightly troubled look crosses Noah's face as he tries to interpret what my son has said. But then he smiles and says he once had a pet starfish that he kept in the bathtub for a week, until it died. Me, too, I want to tell him. But I don't, for he will not care. And in another few seconds he excuses himself.

There are days when Noah seems such a lost soul. And maybe because of the feelings I have for his sister, or because of my own slightly peculiar childhood, I will ignore his indiscretions. He will be allowed to bend a team rule, extend my patience. To him, discipline, any discipline, is the enemy. Other days, though, the flavor is different: he just seems like a punk kid. And I don't care who his sister is or that he has traveled a difficult road. Logic evaporates. Nothing good can come from pretending I did not hear him insult Cy Connell or letting him arrive ten minutes late to practice. There's a certain desperation to his behavior, as if it's the only way he knows, the life he's been handed: a sweater at Christmas instead of a locomotive-train set.

The drive to Zoe's farm is a long, rambling journey through clean, flat acres of freshly tilled prairie land. For much of the time Calvin and I are in a no-passing zone behind an enormous John Deere tractor with red-and-yellow hazard flags flapping at both sides. The tractor is a newer model with an enclosed driver's seat that allows for air-conditioning on hot days. Also, many of the new tractors have tape players, and as I watch the driver through my windshield I cannot tell if his head is bobbing with the movements of the vehicle or to music.

The entrance to Zoe's stable is supposed to be a half mile beyond the crossing of Route 36 and Farland Road, but when we get to the flashing red light that marks the intersection there's a small fork and I don't know which road is Farland. Zoe never mentioned an auxiliary street and I turn back, stopping a mile or so up at a gas station for directions. Calvin and I split a root beer and a package of cheese-and-peanut-butter crackers before we continue, taking the left side of the fork, which is Farland.

The driveway is wooded and long and at its entrance marked by a hollow tree stump painted orange. Calvin sits scout and calls out when he sees the orange tree. As we drive slowly toward the stable, the car pitching unevenly as it sinks into divots and pits along the dirt path, I point at the horizon, where someone is riding a gray-colored horse.

"That's her? That's her horse?"

"I'm not sure, Cal. I can't tell from here."

I hit the horn and Calvin waves, but the person continues riding toward the roll of the earth. Calvin looks perplexed, until I pull around back, beside Zoe's truck, and he sees Zoe bending in front of a wooden fence, a sledgehammer at her side. She has both hands cupped around the base of one of the fence posts and she is rocking it into the soft dirt. Calvin jumps from the car, running to where Zoe is crouched, and throwing both his arms into the sky, as if to say, "Here I am." She stands and touches Calvin on the shoulder.

"And how are you?" she asks, brushing soil from her knees and chest.

"Fine. We just saw a horse over there," Calvin says, looking to his left. "Is it yours?"

"No. That's my friend Jane and her horse."

"Oh."

"My horse is over here." Zoe points to a patch of grass behind the fence she is repairing at a chestnut filly with a white diamond on her nose and white socks on her two hind legs. "This is Willa."

Calvin runs to the fence and props his legs up against its lowest rung, as if he is going to climb it. But Zoe grabs him before I can say anything, telling him the fence is loose and it could slip under his weight. She calls to her horse and then so does Calvin, but Willa is uninterested, grazing alone near the middle of the penned-in pasture.

"Let's try this." Zoe reaches into a paper bag and pulls out several carrots. "Why don't you wave one of these at her."

"Carrots? Horses like carrots?"

"Sure they do."

Calvin holds the carrot between the open space of the fence, swinging it back and forth while calling for Willa to come, as he might call for a dog or Moonie the cat or me. It doesn't take long for the horse to trot over, leaning down close and rolling back her rubbery lips to reveal teeth brown and mossy and each nearly as big as Calvin's hand. She takes the carrot directly from Calvin, who seems completely unafraid, holding on until Willa has a good grip. Not dropping it and jumping back. This impresses both Zoe and me.

"That's good, Calvin," Zoe says. "Most people aren't that brave their first time."

Calvin nods and reaches for another carrot.

Then Zoe looks to me and smiles. "Welcome."

My face turns warm and pink with blood—embarrassed, as if she is aware, has been aware of my thoughts about her since our first meeting.

"You look tired," she says to me, handing Calvin the last of the carrots.

"Good, 'cause I feel tired."

"You'll relax today."

She turns back to Calvin and asks him if he is ready to go for a ride, to which he responds with a precocious "Of course. That's why I'm here."

Zoe prepares the horse, first with a heavy shetland blanket and then with a saddle, which she adjusts by pulling the straps against Willa's firm belly. Calvin stands at Zoe's side the entire time, holding the bridle beside his foot until Zoe takes it to hook into the horse's mouth. When she does this, Willa struggles slightly and Zoe leans close and blows into Willa's nose while massaging the underside of her jawline. Calvin is fascinated by this and Zoe explains her actions. She says that when horses are together, in a field or a stable, they will get real near and breathe into each other's noses. It is almost like a greeting, and when people do it, to try to imitate other horses, it usually has a calming effect on the animal.

After some minor adjustments, Zoe lifts Calvin on the horse and then she climbs into the saddle behind him. The two ride slowly for a few minutes with Calvin holding onto the horn at the front of the saddle, until Zoe reaches over Calvin's arms and allows him to take hold of the reins with her. They break into a trot and then a gallop and I can see Calvin smiling as they turn at the edge of the pasture, before a gate leading out to a larger field, the one that Jane occupies. When they ride off, it is at a brisk pace, but I am not worried about his safety. Oddly, I feel as comfortable with this stranger's arms wrapped around him as I would with my own.

This is part of the life I envisioned for Calvin when I moved us to Kansas, to the very solar plexus of the country. That he be able to breathe in the sweetness of the land, so thick with fragrance it scars his nasal passages and lungs. That he have an appreciation for nature and its majesty and what it can provide. And also for its power. During our first few months in Tarent, late one night, Calvin was awakened by a storm and he called me to his bedside. We pulled apart the drapes shielding his window and watched a twister far on the horizon, flicking awkwardly, resembling a heavy strand of saliva hanging from the sky, waiting to break or be knocked free and fall gently to the ground. The twister never came any closer to us than that, and soon after, Calvin was again asleep, leaving me to roam the rooms of our new house and wonder whether my decision to move us here was the right one.

Zoe and Calvin ride back into the gated corral, their bodies snapping to the rhythm of the horse's steps. Calvin waves when he sees me, but then quickly takes hold again of the reins. Zoe climbs down and reaches for Calvin, who pushes her away, saying that now he wants to ride alone. Before I can tell him he is too young, too inexperienced, Zoe takes the reins around to the front and tells Calvin to hold tight to the horn atop the saddle. Then, slowly, she leads him about the penned-in area. I slide down from my place on the fence and walk at her side.

"It must be hard," Zoe says, loosening her grip slightly on the brown leather straps in her hands.

"What?"

"Raising a son by yourself. Alone. Moving to a new town like this. Changing your life."

"Mmmm."

"You probably don't give it much thought. People never do until it's over. Until afterwards."

"No, I give it plenty of thought. I mean, this is not the life I planned. It's just what happened."

In fact, oddly, the thoughts seemed clearest one night in Ann Arbor when I'd taken a pill to help me sleep. Poured into an easy chair, almost logy, I suddenly remembered the oafishness of junior-high dances: huddled against the cafeteria wall until, scratchy with adrenaline, I mustered the courage to ask some girl to dance the final song; *Stairway to Heaven*, or *Free Bird*. Then, only then, I wanted it to last longer—forever, even. And Calvin's childhood seems the same to me; it's not something I can sneak up on. Soon the song will end . . . and I will be left with quiet.

"I know things about you," she says, turning to face me directly. "More things than you think I know. More than you know about me."

"How? From Noah?"

"No. Well, some. But mostly from Peg Blyth. The two of us take an art class together. Pottery."

Peg is Richard Blyth's wife.

"Are they nice things?"

"Yes. She likes you very much. She says you make excellent matzo balls."

I smile. "Calvin likes them. I dot them with red food coloring and he pretends they're baseballs, that he's eating a baseball."

Zoe takes Calvin around one last time before she leads Willa in to be hosed off, brushed, and fed. While Calvin and I are waiting, we sit at a picnic table shaded by a twisted maple tree, its cross-hatching of branches forming a natural gazebo. Calvin watches as I unpack two shopping bags full of prepared food we bought earlier in the day, after basketball practice. I lay out a cardboard bucket of fried chicken, tin trays wobbly with potato salad and coleslaw, corn bread, carrot and celery sticks wrapped in cellophane, half a blueberry pie (Calvin's favorite), a carton of lemonade, paper plates and cups, plastic silverware, and napkins, which I weight with three unsliced tomatoes. Calvin makes a face when he sees the tomatoes and I tell him he doesn't have to eat any if he has enough celery.

"If I promise to eat a lot of cel'ree, can I have pie first?"

"No."

He doesn't press the issue, because he knows the rules. Also, because he is pleased as a puppy after his ride. So excited that his face blazes a comic-book crimson.

After things are set, we take our places on one of the benches, Calvin's feet swinging back and forth behind the newfound heft of his boots. I can feel him staring up at me, hard, and I know what he is going to ask next. He is going to ask me if he can have a horse of his own, like Willa. One that he can ride whenever he wants, without us having to call Zoe to arrange it or without her perched up there on the saddle behind him. But he doesn't ask for a horse. He doesn't ask for anything.

"I'm gonna thank Zoe when she comes here," he says, turning his attention toward the barn. "I liked riding on Willa."

I place my hand over the soft muscles of his shoulder and give a gentle, short squeeze—to let him know I am pleased. He wriggles free, leaning back and then sliding across the table, flicking his hand as if shooing me away. At the same time Zoe calls out "Fellas," and both Calvin and I look up as she snaps our picture with a Polaroid camera. The photograph spits out from the front and she gives it to Calvin.

"Watch it develop."

"Huh?"

"I don't think he's ever seen a Polaroid," I say.

"Oh. Keep looking at that and tell me what you see, Cal."

Zoe makes her way around to the other side of the table and then, before sitting down, says, "This really looks terrific." She unfastens her hair and shakes it out behind her before tying it beneath a soiled red bandana.

"What can I serve you?" she asks.

"Let me," I say, standing and taking a paper plate from the stack. She points and I serve her two drumsticks, some potato salad, and coleslaw. As I pour out three glasses of lemonade, she slices up a tomato, using the dull, serrated edge of a plastic knife. For the first couple of strokes the tomato sags into mushy wedges, until Zoe gets the hang of it and begins sawing instead of pushing.

"Hey," Calvin says softly, almost to himself.

I peer over his shoulder and watch as the photo finishes its metamorphosis from ghostlike shapes, clouded and grainy, to the familiar colors and contours of Calvin's and my body. In the picture, Calvin is nearly horizontal, his arms outstretched and pushing me away. My right arm is raised, and although I know it was because I was reaching for him, it actually looks as if I'm trying to strike him. Sometimes even the truths of photographs can deceive. They can turn anything on itself.

Packed away in a padded envelope somewhere in the back of one of my closets, or in the basement, is a framed picture of my father and me taken shortly after

I turned one. My father is standing on the top step outside our new house in Lakeshire, holding me high on his chest like a priceless vase. We are both grinning and I have imagined, on viewing the snapshot later in life, that people must have thought the two of us were quite close. Not only from pictures, but from certain actions, greasy and slick. In public, my father always stressed how much his family meant to him, how none of his success would have been possible without the support of his loving wife and son. At games, he sat us directly behind the team bench, and although in later years I was often absent, my mother always attended, dressed in a matching skirt and blazer, her hands clutching a stuffed Eagle mascot against her lap. Truthfully, though, we saw more of my father during those two-odd hours pacing the sideline than we ever saw of him at home.

Once, when he and I got into a late-night argument over something I can no longer remember, or perhaps simply something I have selectively chosen to forget, I cornered him on his notion of familial love and he threw an ashtray at me, claiming I was a wise-ass bastard. The ashtray broke into two neat pieces at my feet with a dull snap. I told him I might be a wise-ass, but I most certainly wasn't a bastard. That unfortunately I knew exactly who my father was. Which is something I have tried to keep in mind while raising Calvin: that he always knows his father.

At the moment, Calvin's father is watching Zoe dip her fried chicken into runny white coleslaw broth before she takes a bite. Calvin is sitting quietly at the end of the table, waving his photo out at his side like an imaginary wing in between bites of food. He very much wants to try the camera himself, but Zoe will not allow it until he finishes his supper. Neither of them even cast so much as a glance in my direction when this decree was made, which pleases me to no uncertain end.

Right now, an outsider might say we have the look of a happy family. Again, I am filled with pleasure. Let my son at least pretend to know what that feels like on this crisp, cloudless afternoon when he dreamed of being a cowboy.

SEVEN

Calvin has hooked his necktie through the window of his toy dump truck and now he is using it like a leash, dragging the truck from kitchen to living room. He is wearing only a white dress shirt, unbuttoned. His gray flannel slacks are lying empty at the foot of the stairs, with one small brown shoe turned over nearby and the other sandwiched between the couch's seat cushions. When I call for him to finish getting dressed he says he is hungry, that he wants a bowl of cereal or some licorice. I'm not sure where he got the idea for licorice, but I tell him he can have a cookie when he is presentable. Upon hearing this, he simply shrugs and leads his truck through the kitchen again and to the back door, where he stands straight-limbed, glaring at the placid land behind our house.

The telephone rings and I adjust my own tie in the phone's silver cradle. It is Kate calling from Dallas. She says she's been back in the States for three days but she is still battling jet lag. Before she can ask, I tell her I never got around to giving Calvin her postcard, that it is on my dresser and I am sorry, I have no excuse. She sighs, her breath coming hard through the receiver. Then, in a quiet, unexpected tone, she tells me it is all right.

"Really, I just wanted Calvin to know I was thinking about him," she says.

I am silent for a spell, looking up at Calvin, who is rubbing his nose against the screen door. Cupping my palm over the mouthpiece, I ask him what he is doing. He says his nose itches and that the "scratchy part" of the door feels good.

"Is everything okay?" Kate asks.

"Sure. Sure it is."

"Gordon, do you think I could talk to him—just for a few minutes?"

I tell her she can, but that we're in a hurry, so she should try to keep it short. Then I call Calvin to the telephone.

"It's Mom," I say, sliding a chair over for him to stand on while he talks. He is not used to getting telephone calls.

"Gramma?"

"No. Mom—your mom. Kate."

"Oh," he says, taking the phone from me as he climbs on the chair. In a very straight, self-assured voice he says, "Hello."

His dump truck sits below the sink and I walk over and unfasten the necktie, smoothing it out against my chest while he talks. A fine, red line bisects his naked belly and I can see it darken as he pulls the telephone cord back and forth in a raking motion. He says "Uh-huh" a couple of times and then laughs. After a few more minutes he says, "Yeah, that would be good," and then, "Well, we have to go to th' game now." He pitches his shoulder and I wave for him to say goodbye, to hand the phone back to me.

"What game is he talking about?" she asks.

Briefly, I tell her about my coaching and wait for her to question me about Calvin, about who watches over him or what he does while I'm at the gymnasium. But she does not inquire about those things at all. Instead, she asks how everything is with me.

"Oh, I'm all right," I say.

"That's good, Gordon. Really. That's good."

Calvin remains at my side, his hand clutching a roll of fabric under the seat of my pants, as he does when he is nervous or when we're in a crowd.

"What I wanted to ask was about coming up to see him," she says quickly, forcing the words together. "To see you both."

"God," I start, and then fall still.

"Really, I wouldn't get in the way. I'd only stay for a couple of days, at some hotel nearby, and I promise I wouldn't be a pest."

"Kate, this is kind of a busy time for us here. Let me think about it, okay?"

"Sure," she says. "I'll call you next week."

Before she hangs up, she has one last question, one thing she forgot to ask. "What's he dressing up as for Halloween?"

It is a subject Calvin and I haven't thought much about. And because I do not want Kate to think me negligent, and because the holiday is in only two days, I say the first thing that comes into my mind. Actually, the second. The first was a fireman; the second is cereal.

"Cereal? Like in Cheerios or something?"

"Yeah."

"That's certainly—"

"Kate, we gotta go."

When I turn back to face the open part of the kitchen, Calvin is perched on the countertop swabbing waves of peanut butter out of the jar. I pull him down and wipe his face and hands with a dish towel.

"Look," I say, turning his hands palms-down. "You've got peanut butter under your fingernails."

He cocks his head, not sure how to respond.

"If you get hungry during the game, just bite your nails."

Not long before Kate and I became serious about each other, I slept with one of her friends. It was accidental, almost—a drunken groping, wrestling naked on the windowsill, desk, and toilet tank.

And Kate found out. We sat in her bedroom, both blinking away salt leaking from our tear ducts. Neither of us wanted this thing between us to end, we were so close to love. She leaned over and I thought she meant to kiss me on the side of my face. Instead, she rolled up the sleeve of my T-shirt and started slugging me, hard, like a guy, near where my arm connected to my shoulder.

She hit me maybe ten, fifteen times in the same spot.

"That'll bruise," she said, once she'd finished and was rubbing her hand between her thighs.

I nodded, refusing to touch the throbbing welt on my arm.

"Leave now," she said. "And don't call me again until the bruise has disappeared completely."

When I finally came over again, nine days later, she made me remove my shirt and she checked my arm in the light for the faintest of markings. Then she punched me one last time and told me we'd never discuss this again.

Calvin and I sit quietly in the corner of the school parking lot, me peering through the windshield as people begin filing into the gymnasium, Calvin picking at a loose thread near his left knee. After five minutes or so, Noah Ward enters, followed closely by Zoe. It makes me feel good that she has come to the game, even if it is only to watch her brother play—although I don't think that's the case. She is wearing a plaid skirt and dark thigh-high leg warmers.

A few days ago, I returned home to find Calvin sitting on the floor of his bedroom trying to yank a pair of green tights onto his legs. He had stolen the tights from Meg, slipped them into his sack before Charlotte dropped him at the house. Something about watching him lying there, fumbling, the tights tangled about his calves like cabbage plants, repulsed me. "You're crazy," I said, walking to his side. "You little screwed-up . . ." Then I stepped on his ankle, forcefully, causing him to holler and squirm. It lasted only an instant, until I removed my foot. There are so many moments when it seems I am still examining the weight and texture of parenthood. Sometimes, there's just a meanness we act upon—the same evil streak that once forced Mrs. Grafton, the kindest woman on the planet, into making nasty, distorted faces at her mother, who was suffering from Alzheimer's disease. "It was inexcusable," said Mrs. Grafton later, over a glass of gin in my kitchen. "I scared her to death and I don't even know why. I guess I just wanted to make some impression, some contact. Like I was asking, 'Are you in there? Can you hear me?' "

Finally, when I'm lost well among my thoughts and have forgotten about Calvin, he turns to me and says, "Could we go in now?"

Last night it rained heavy and there is a large kidney-shaped puddle of mud between my car and the back door to the gym. Although he begins to whine, I hoist Calvin over my shoulder and carry him toward my office to preserve his best pair of shoes. We leave our coats and I sort through some papers on my clipboard before walking down the hallway that leads to the gymnasium floor. The girls' varsity team is finishing its game with Fairview and I poke my head in to see the scoreboard. Tarent is ahead by six, with slightly under four minutes remaining. Calvin tries to look inside, too, but I pull him back and direct him to the locker room.

The boys are standing around in various states of undress, some of them talking, laughing. In a far corner Pat Booth is lacing a new pair of sneakers, while Chris Rayles sits at his side, pointing at a picture in a magazine, trying to get Pat to look up. Eric Shaw is sprinkling powder on his feet, kneading it in with the heel of his palm. Calvin rushes to Peter Sawyer, who is pulling at the armpits of his jersey to loosen it. He slips it on and then lets Calvin grab hold and dangle from it as he stands.

"You look kind of nervous," Peter says, turning to me with Calvin clinging to his torso like a suckling orangutan.

"Are you?" I ask.

"A little."

"Yeah, me too. A little. I suppose that's only natural, though."

Peter nods and then lowers Calvin to the ground. Ned Morrow comes up behind me and asks if he can have another jersey number, he has decided he doesn't like the one he's been assigned.

"You'll have to wear it for this game. I'll look and see what I've got for next time."

A boy I've never seen before comes in to tell me the girls' game has ended and we have to take the floor for warm-up in fifteen minutes.

There is nothing else I can tell them, I think, my eyes skipping from face to face. Noah spins a ball on his finger, slapping at it occasionally with his free hand to keep it moving.

My father might have given them something they could use, told them how much this game meant, how it will set the tone for the rest of the season. How they should reach down inside for that something extra, if need be, and not let him or the school down. But, most important, not to let themselves down. I will not speak of these things. For, after all, they are simply children.

"Have some fun," I say.

They are waiting for more, but there is nothing else. Only a small smile from Calvin as he follows me out the swinging door. The first time I hear their voices again, I am halfway down the corridor to the gym. And even then, they sound stunted and unclear.

Calvin reaches the bench before me, climbing up to greet Zoe, who is seated in the bleachers behind him. I'm walking slowly around the court, taking it all in like a long, sweet breath. A couple of cheerleaders run past, digging through their purses as they reach for the pay telephone. The air smells of warm, buttered popcorn and hot dogs, which rotate on a spit behind one of the school's mathematics teachers at the concession stand. Against the walls at either end of the floor are hand-lettered signs painted by the school's pep committee. *The Trojans Will Triumph*, says one. Another has an enormous red Trojan holding a rather meek-looking wolf in his armored fist. It reads: *Rip the Wolves.*

There seems to be a relatively good-sized crowd, with most of the bleacher seats taken. Poised near the scorer's table, wearing a flannel shirt and tweed blazer, is Lyle Anderson, the man who rented Calvin and me our house. He is talking to Jess Thomas, the school's principal and scoreboard operator. As I approach them, Lyle grabs my bicep and gives it a gentle squeeze as he wishes me luck. I thank him and take a drink from one of the water bottles beneath our bench. Calvin sees this and calls for a drink of his own. But once I hand him the bottle he begins squirting it randomly, sending squiggly, toothpaste-fine bursts of water across his legs and on the floor in front of him.

"That's enough," I say, taking a towel and wiping up the damp spot beyond the bench. I wave to Zoe and she smiles back, holding up her right hand and crossing her fingers.

"For luck," she says, so softly I can barely make out the words.

Then Jess Thomas sounds a loud buzzer that causes Calvin to jump. Carbon Springs comes out first, immediately breaking into two single-file lines for a lay-up drill at the opposite end of the court. Shortly thereafter, Tarent follows suit and the crowd erupts with applause. This is the best part of the game, I remember my father once saying under his breath as I stood at his side. He meant the endless possibilities, the prickly energy popping from each nerve ending. It is taking forever, I think, pacing in front of the bench while the boys change from lay-ups to jump shots. From behind, Zoe reaches down and hands me a stick of chewing gum.

"It'll help you relax," she says.

"What makes you think I need relaxing?"

"That," she responds, pointing to a game program I have nearly twisted in two with my right hand.

The first basket is scored by Eric Shaw, who intercepts the opening tip and dribbles freely to the foul line, where he hits a jumper. Sitting motionless, hands facedown on my thighs, I watch them set up on defense. They begin in a two-three zone and I yell out for them to put their hands up. Quickly, it becomes apparent that

Carbon Springs is overmatched and by halftime Tarent is ahead by 16 points.

There is much of the same in the second half and I ease into the role of fan instead of coach. I no longer walk through the plays in my mind; now I simply enjoy the game. Late, after much of the crowd has already begun to leave, I glance down the bench and realize that Cy Connell is the only player who hasn't been in yet. I call him over and tell him to replace Noah.

When he does, Noah reluctantly grabs a towel and turns to me. "I only need one more bucket," he says. "I've got 18 points."

"Cy has no points," I say.

Noah shrugs, and almost instinctively, sickened by his lack of compassion, his absence of decency, I swing my arm toward his forehead. Casually, as if scattering birdseed. Already he has moved down the bench and I strike air, only air. No one notices; it appears as if I am simply signaling a play or stretching my arm, awkwardly, from deep at the shoulder. But, really, I had wanted to hit Noah, intending to slap him hard with my open hand. My mouth turns arid and bitter as tobacco. "*That's* it," I say to myself, pacing along a small rectangle near the scorer's table. Deck him. Pop him good, in front of his teammates and teachers and sister and your own goddam son.

So now the fire comes in a tidy box, lapping at sides charred and crooked with damage. Thoughts plead for safety: If you really want, slug him with a roll of quarters curled in your palm, the cartilage in his nose splintering into bloody hangnails of gristle. Stand over his twitching body, cursing, hands pink and jagged. Better: Kick him solid in the ribs and chest with steel-toe workboots. He won't mouth off again; he'll never wear his freakin' earring or show up late for practice. This *cannot* be me, I think, terrified, scratching the flaky skin at my elbow. Not even for an instant. Ugly and raw. It's only in my head, all in my head. But what's to keep the hair-trigger soldered tight?

A sickness I will not be able to vomit away.

Before turning my attention again toward the game, I look down the bench, frightened—I look to meet Noah's gaze and apologize with a gesture or nod for almost striking him. He does not see me, his head twisted back to find familiar faces in the stands. He does not know that sometimes even coaches, even fathers, fill with awful, hateful thoughts. Especially fathers.

In his two minutes and fourteen seconds of playing time, Cy doesn't exactly distinguish himself. He is called for traveling and once he almost throws a pass into the concession stand. Still, when the buzzer sounds he is the first person I go to, slapping him on the butt and telling him he played well.

It's nice to be undefeated as a coach, even if it is only one game. Certainly, I suppose, it's more satisfying than being 0 and 1. Walking toward my office, I am congratulated by several people. One of them is Calvin, who, leaving Zoe's side, walks over and uncomfortably raises his hand.

"Good game," he says, peering back toward Zoe.

"Thanks, pal."

"She made me say it."

"That's all right. It's a very nice thing to do."

He shrugs and then tells me that he is hungry.

"We're going to get a quick bite to eat," I say to Zoe. "You wanna come with?"

She says she would, but she has promised to let her brother use the truck.

"I think we could manage giving you a ride home," I say, tapping Calvin on the head with my forefinger.

Sitting behind a cheeseburger that nearly eclipses his entire face, Calvin reaches up for a handful of french fries. I had asked the waitress for a booster chair, but Calvin complained, insisting he did not need one. Zoe is talking about the tendons marbling a horse's leg, how the ones down low are often as thin and fragile as lace. However, at the moment I am not listening. Instead, I'm watching as Calvin carefully, deliberately, grabs his burger, the weight of his forearms resting flush against the plate. Slow like porridge, the dish slides forward, hitting Calvin in the chest before landing upside down on his lap. Instantly he begins to wail, pushing himself back from the table and allowing the plate and its substance to roll off his shins and on the floor.

"Oh, now stop that," I say, lifting my head to assess the damage. "Didn't I ask for a high chair? Didn't I tell you the food was too far?"

From the corner of my eye, I can see Zoe wants to say something, to intercede. Maybe she wants to tell me that I'm doing this all wrong, that I should not be so hard on him. Maybe she wants me to wait until I get home to chastise him, wait until then to explain tables and height and the length of a little boy's arms. But finally she is only quiet, taking a small, quick mouthful of her meat loaf.

"Let's take you to the bathroom to get cleaned."

He does not want me to come along, saying he can do it himself. Tonight he is suddenly feeling very independent.

"You'll see," I say to Zoe in a sarcastic tone. "Someday you'll have kids of your own."

She smiles and we both watch Calvin disappear around the corner as a busboy begins cleaning the scraps of spilled cheeseburger.

"This must be something that feels nice to you," she says. "I mean tonight. The game. Having Calvin with you to see it all."

Indeed it does, although it's not something I had given much thought to until now. Zoe leans back and the orange, muted light sets her hair ablaze.

"You're good with him," I say.

"Really, he's good with me." She pauses to take a bite of mashed potatoes. "I like watching the two of you together. Like the other day, after we were finished riding, he came right up and buried his head in your stomach. But not because he was unhappy or embarrassed or tired or anything like that—just as sort of a greeting. And then after, I watched you both walk to the picnic table and you reached down and handed him the napkins to hold, to carry. So he would feel as if he was making a contribution. We never had that in our home. There was only a lot of tension."

"There was a lot of that when I was growing up, too."

"My mother was an alcoholic—she died when Noah was thirteen. My father just didn't know how to deal with her, or us. He still doesn't, for that matter. He's a good man, good at heart, but he doesn't understand . . ." She trails off, rubbing her chin with her napkin while she thinks of the right words. "I guess what he doesn't understand is *life*—or a life when it's different from his own. That I could want to be a veterinarian and not a housewife. Or that Noah might actually want to go away to college to study business or law or literature or anything other than growing goddam corn and wheat.

"Sometimes it seems so peculiar to me that a man could live fifty-eight years and know nothing else of life, of the world, than what's in his own back yard. But other times I don't think it's odd at all. When I was young I used to lie in bed at night and wonder, Who's gonna save *me*?" Carefully, she places her fork down at the left side of her plate as if it had not yet been moved. "Forty-five minutes after my mother's funeral, my father went back to working his fields."

Pursing my lips, I prepare to tell her how three years after my father's funeral my mother still hasn't gone back to work. Not because she is weighted by grief, but quite to the contrary. She has spent a good deal of that time traveling, painting, reading. Shortly after my father's death, I found my mother sitting on her bed with her back to the door, making delicate yelping sounds. I came up from behind and laid my hand across her shoulder, telling her things would be all right. But when she turned to face me, I could see she wasn't crying at all. She was laughing.

She apologized, saying she could not help herself, and, truthfully, she had never been happier. Really, she said, reaching for my arm, she never thought she would feel this free, this liberated again. She stood up and held me for a long time, not like a mother holding a son, but with her body pressed close, tight against mine, and a stranger's sour breath on my neck. Then, before we went back downstairs, she told me that my father was not a bad person, he was simply someone who should not have been a husband.

This I do not tell Zoe, though, because rather suddenly Calvin returns, not much cleaner than before. He climbs back on his chair and I give him half my hamburger, telling him to be careful.

"Is there mustard on this?" he asks.

"No, there's not mustard on it."

"I want it."

"No, you don't want it. You don't like mustard on your hamburger. You never had it before."

"I want it now."

"Calvin, just eat the burger."

After he begins I grab some fries and place them on a butter dish, sliding it between us.

"You want to come over to our place for Halloween?" I ask Zoe. Calvin glances up, but he is not quite sure what Halloween means. This will be his first season trick-or-treating.

"Oh, I'd love to. But I'm working at Cale's."

"Maybe we'll stop by there."

"That'd be great. What's he going . . ." She stops and leans down toward Calvin, inhaling a heady breath through her nostrils. "Do you smell anything?" she asks me. "Kind of like piss."

"Now . . ." I take a sniff. "Yeah."

Zoe peels back the front of Calvin's shirttail, revealing a damp, tennis-ball-sized stain on his upper thigh.

"Jesus!" I say. "Calvin, did you go to the bathroom in your pants?"

"No."

Still holding his half of the burger, he twists his body to free Zoe's grip.

"Then what's that?"

He does not answer, instead laying the burger directly on the Formica table.

"Get up," I say, pulling him off his seat and around toward me. "Let me see this."

Touching the stain, I can feel a hard lump beneath the cloth of his trousers. I reach into his pocket and pull out a thick, waxy urinal puck. Oddly enough, I am relieved.

"What are you doing with this?"

Zoe is trying hard not to laugh, but she is not having much success and she walks over to the front counter for a toothpick.

"It was in there," he starts, pointing back to the bathroom. "And we don't have one, so I jus' . . ."

He is sincere. Taking the puck, I wrap it in a napkin. "What is with you and toilets?"

Of course, he does not know the answer to this. He

is picking at fries over my shoulder as I kneel, diluting the stain with water.

As we drive down Mercer, Calvin sitting tall and odorous on Zoe's lap, the windshield fills with droplets of icy rain. But after one wave of the wipers it is clear again for the rest of the ride, for the rest of the evening. Zoe lives on Hillside, in an apartment above a record store. We park on the street and I leave Calvin in the car, lying across the front seat, while I walk Zoe to her door.

"Really, you don't have to do this," she says, pulling her keys from the breast pocket of her jacket.

We step together the ten or so feet from the curb to her doorway, arms locked. Nervously, she tugs at the waistband of her sweater, bunching it above the hemline. My hands run down past her elbows, past her forearms, past her wrists before letting our left fingers lock together. She is holding the keys in her right hand, jagged and cold, pressed awkwardly between our palms. Laying my forehead on her shoulder, I push her flush against the building and then lift up to kiss her square on the mouth.

At first her lips are stiff and dry as chalk. It doesn't take long for them to moisten, slick with saliva. Holding her face in my hands, I trace the outline of her mouth with my tongue and slowly, cautiously, I move it along the inside of her lower lip. Then we both pull back, ghosts of breath dispersing above our heads.

"That was nice," she says.

"It's been awhile."

We hug and as she slides the bridge of her nose down my jawline, she says, "I'd better go." But before we part, she leans in close, the linty fuzz of her cheek brushing my earlobe.

Lying against our back screen door is a large padded envelope with four dollars' worth of 20-cent stamps pasted on its upper right corner. The parcel is from my mother and I am slightly encouraged by the fact that I did not have to sign for it. I allow Calvin to take it upstairs with him, but I tell him he must get ready for bed before opening it.

When I enter his room he is sitting on the floor wearing one of my white undershirts and his pajama bottoms, the torn package at his feet.

"This," he says, holding up two colorful leather belts. "It's just this."

The belts have geometric Native American beadwork sewn into their backsides and I take the larger of the two and pull it around my waist.

"Looks like it fits," I say, turning to model it for Calvin.

"There's no manna-war or nothin'," he says, pawing through the ripped remains of the envelope. "But hey . . ."

He grabs his belt and walks over to the window, futilely trying to pull it open.

"We could use them for the roof," he says.

"Maybe."

"Yeah. Let's use 'em now."

"No, now is time for you to go to sleep."

"I'm not tired," he says, letting the belt dangle so he can kick at the buckle. "Could we . . ."

I am prepared to say no, until I think about what Zoe said earlier, about how this night must feel good—especially to have Calvin with me. Someday I will never want it to end.

"Okay. But only for a few minutes."

What my son is anxious for is some time on the roof, sitting on the long, wide ledge outside his window, staring off into the horizon. The first time the two of us climbed out there, a week or so after we moved into the house, it was completely by accident. He had pushed one of his toy cars onto the ledge and had gone out to retrieve it when I came into his room. Frantic, I climbed out after him, but instead of yelling, I hugged him against my rib cage, like a football, and the two of us sat there looking at the vast spread of land as it climbed and dipped. On subsequent trips, I had fastened two belts together and slipped them first through a handle on the shutter and then around Calvin. Although he didn't quite understand, I told him it was like a window washer's rig.

After we get settled, Calvin closest to the window, with the two beaded belts slung tightly across his chest and beneath his armpits, I push a pair of socks onto his fingers so he will stay warm. In the short time since we have been home, a light dusting of snow has fallen, making the ground glow white and the trees resemble coral.

"We didn't see this," says Calvin of the snow.

"I know. It happened while you were getting ready for bed."

He lets out a sigh of approval and I reach across him, pointing at a runaway band of wheat that wanders from Speck Beattie's field, crossing behind our dirt basketball court before stopping dead at the toolshed beside Mrs. Grafton's porch. The sprained stalks reach up from underneath the patchy snow, appearing almost auburn in the darkness.

"From up here it looks like a river," I say, more to myself than to Calvin. Again I remember something Zoe mentioned this evening: how as a child she used to lie in bed at night and wonder who was going to save her. "I have those thoughts, too," I murmur into the side of Calvin's head. But he is no longer listening, instead pressing his sock-covered hand into the snow and then placing its surface against his cheek, just to feel the coldness.

EIGHT

Sitting cross-legged atop my desk, Meg Cooper and Calvin use yellow crayons to color a bowl of cornflakes I have drawn in pencil on a large sheet of white cardboard. This is going to be the front side of Calvin's costume. Meg is dressed as a princess, wearing a plastic-and-rhinestone tiara that has slipped down toward her forehead, now resembling a visor. On the floor at their side, Joyce Ives has spread out several pages of newspaper and is carving a pumpkin with a grapefruit knife, saving the seeds in two coffee mugs. Across the room, Rob silently leafs through a magazine, occasionally looking up to see if we're all still here.

As I shield a legal pad on my lap, I consider devising a payment schedule to Gooland's that Rob and Joyce can handle, but instead sketch out several basketball plays from memory, plays that were my father's. My highly trained attorney's mind descends to a scribble of dashes, zigzags, and arrows across faded blue notebook lines reserved for deep thoughts—deeper, anyway, than run, catch, shoot.

"See, you bake these and then you can eat them," Joyce says to the kids. Meg nods, reaching for another color crayon.

"Meg, honey," I say, "there are no green cornflakes."

"What about rotten ones? Those could be green."

"We don't want any rotten ones on Calvin's costume. Let's just stick with the yellow for now."

"They're not really yellow, either," says Rob.

Both Calvin and Meg look up, worried expressions crossing their faces.

"Yeah, I know," I whisper to Rob. "But this box of crayons didn't come with a cornflake color." Then I turn toward my desk. "It's okay, yellow is close enough."

The two continue their work and Joyce flips a shiny seed into Rob's glass of soda, shaking her head and saying something about his lacking sensitivity. Rob is leaning over, adjusting the tuner on a transistor radio, trying to get a country-and-western station from Manhattan.

"The reception in here is the pits," he announces, lifting the radio to his ear.

"Maybe you'd have more luck if you went outside," says Joyce. "Try standing in the street."

He doesn't respond, and then, after a minute, he tells her that this morning, while she was still asleep, he did two loads of laundry. He says it's folded in baskets beside the dryer and he will carry it upstairs when they get home. Then he rises and leaves the room.

"He's trying," Joyce says softly, to me. "He made me oatmeal for breakfast. It was bad, *really* bad. Lumpy. And he didn't mix it enough, so there were still dry flecks of oat. But . . . lots of women don't have men who will make them oatmeal when it's cold out."

"We eat oatmeal," says Meg, suddenly.

"I know you do, sweetheart."

After Joyce and Rob leave, I dress Calvin and Meg in the rest of their costumes. Meg wants to wear plastic high-heeled shoes, but it has been wet out and I insist she put on boots.

"No princess has these," she says, disgustedly kicking the boot into the middle of the room.

"Some do."

"I don't think so," says Calvin.

"What do you know about princesses, anyway?" I ask him.

"Some things."

"No things."

"I know 'bout the frog."

"That's right, you do. What else?"

"They drink tea," says Meg.

"Really?"

"Uh-huh."

"And they ride horses," shouts Calvin.

"Yes, sometimes they do."

Then I know what he is going to ask next.

"Hey, maybe we could get Zoe's horse for us to ride."

"A cereal box on a horse?" says Meg, scrunching her nose in disapproval.

"That could be. Like maybe the princess wants to take some food along with her."

"It doesn't matter because we can't do it anyway," I say. "Zoe is working tonight. But we'll go see her later."

"Is she with her horse?" asks Calvin.

"No."

"Then I don't want to see her."

"Me neither," says Meg.

"Come on, now. That's not nice."

Taking Calvin by the shoulder, I string the sandwich-board cereal box onto him, making sure to tie knots in three places on both sides. Straddling the arm of the couch, near the doorway, Meg is prodding the jack-o'-lantern with her scepter.

"Are we gonna carry this with us?" she asks.

"No, we're going to stick it in the front window of the office for everyone to see."

Meg gives a nod of approval and then Calvin waddles over to her, his knees knocking the underside of the cardboard.

"I don't want to be cereal," he says.

"It's too late now."

"I wanna be a princess! Look, she gets a wand and I get nothing."

"If you behave, you'll get a big bag full of treats."

Then they are quiet and I lead them into the waiting room, where I place the jack-o'-lantern on a coffee table and slide it in front of the window. As we walk toward the car, I peer back, asking, "Doesn't that look good?" But neither answers.

For the first several houses Calvin is numb, bewildered by the prospect, the reality of receiving free candy from people simply for ringing their doorbells. He wants to unwrap it, eat it immediately, and go back again and again. But I explain that after he is finished trick-or-treating he may have one item tonight and then one—and only one—every day until he has emptied the bag. When I tell him this, Meg lets out a little sigh, as if to say, "We'll polish off the whole stash inside three days."

The flat, newly paved eastern stretch of Eliot Drive is the best place to go door to door, claims Charlotte Cooper. They have closed off the street to allow children to walk right down its well-lighted center. Every so often Calvin and Meg pause to stare at an especially ghoulish or grotesque costume, and it is then that I bend over to remind them it is all pretend, like we see on television or in the movies.

After we have collected booty from houses on both sides of the street, I direct the two of them back toward the car.

"Can we go again?" Calvin asks.

"No, that's not allowed. One time through."

"How about if we go to another place?" says Meg.

"Oh, I don't think so. Look at all the candy you both have," I say, lifting up Calvin's quite full shopping bag. "Where are you going to put more?"

They look at each other and then Calvin suggests they dump their candy on the backseat of the car to make room.

"No. We're going to see Zoe. Maybe she'll have something for you."

In the square front window of Cale's there is a jack-o'-lantern painted on orange construction paper that I am sure Zoe created. Above, in cutout letters from the same paper, are the words *Happy Halloween*. Inside, crepe-paper ribbons of orange and black hang in large loops from the ceiling, with store-bought rubber spiders and bats suspended randomly on strings of various lengths. On the left side of the room, behind the bar, Zoe is serving drinks dressed in her black turtleneck and black jeans. She is also wearing heavy black eyeliner and lipstick and a pointed witch's hat.

"Hey, look at Zoe," I say. "Doesn't she look great?"

Meg shrugs. Calvin has walked over to the jukebox and is standing beside it, his face glowing in artificial blue-and-red light. I lead them both over to the bar, lifting them onto stools. Calvin cannot sit down in his costume, so I slip it off and lean it against the brass foot rail.

"Howdy," Zoe says. "Did you get a lot of candy?"

Meg nods as Calvin begins eating candy corn from a peanut dish.

"You look *very* pretty, Meg. And I loved you, Mr. Cornflake. I saw your costume the minute you walked in the door."

I tap them both between the shoulder blades and they mumble thank yous.

"And what are you supposed to be?" Zoe asks me.

"An exhausted father. Trick-or-treat."

She hands me a bottle of beer. As we talk, people come over to question Meg and Calvin about their costumes and their candy. One man apologizes for giving away his last package of chewing gum and hands the two of them a dollar apiece. Finally, we leave Zoe to her work.

"Why don't you tip her?" I whisper to Calvin and Meg. "Leave her a piece of candy."

Reluctantly, they both surrender something: Calvin a miniature Milky Way bar, and Meg a Saran-wrapped candy apple. They drop the items on the bar and then the three of us wave our goodbyes from the front door.

Once the car has reached a stop in our drive, after we have taken Meg home, Calvin bolts to the far side of the porch. I call out to him, but he only tells me to wait, that he has seen something. At first I think this is some sort of ploy Meg has told him about, a way to hide his candy. But then he lets out a loud, shrill howl, and from where I am standing, in the scattered spokes of light beside the stairs, I can see him lying flat on his back with his legs kicking against the bushes. The stench is immediate.

"Oh, Cal," I say, running to his side.

He has been sprayed, rather directly, by a skunk. His hands, palms down, move rapidly over his chest as he tries to wipe the scent off.

"That's not going to do it," I say, using the placards of his costume to fan the air away.

After a moment more he begins to cry and I reach down and take him by the arm, leading him to the porch, where I seat him on the swing.

"Stay here for a minute."

He complains about the cold, but I tell him it won't be long—I'll be right back. What I want, really, is to leave him there, alone. To climb into my bed and sleep long and soundly and awaken tomorrow morning in an empty house with Calvin clean and scentless and somewhere safe and faraway. It's the same feeling I get some days when I wish the womb of basketball practice could last another hour or so. Then I drive around to escape, however fleeting, escape from Calvin, escape from this life that surely must be borrowed. I am not awful, I tell myself, only reaching blindly—fingertips exposed—for familiar contours, some groove I will eventually recognize.

I plunge a can opener into the side of a quart of tomato juice—a can I was saving for some special Sunday morning I hoped to turn soggy with Bloody Marys. When I pull loose the opener from the barbed aluminum lid, gritty red juice spills to the floor.

Maybe the odor has made me lightheaded, but I seem incapable of thinking straight. There are no more paper towels and I can't find a sponge. The puddle becomes a tiger and then a staple gun before finally reaching the soles of my shoes. I call Zoe at Cale's and she tells me not to fret. They are beginning to clear out and she will see if someone can fill in for her behind the bar.

I wrap Calvin in an old, dirty blanket and move to the opposite end of the porch, where the two of us wait for Zoe. I make an exception and allow him to eat more than one piece of candy, but after his second bite he grows sickened by the smell and throws the chocolate at his feet.

"It was a skunk," I say, solemnly. "Don't ever go near one of those again."

"I thought it was Moonie."

We don't say anything for a long while, with Calvin rocking himself in the swing, his nose and mouth covered by a corner of blanket.

"Maybe some things children just need to be told," I finally say. "Little things fathers might never think to tell them until it's too late or until it passes randomly through their minds. You didn't know about skunks, huh?"

He shakes his head, simply.

More silence passes until it is broken by the sound of Zoe's truck grinding to a halt. Briefly, she sits behind the wheel staring up at the two of us as we stare back.

"You stink!" she shouts to Calvin from the driveway. She is carrying a brown paper bag.

"*You* stink," he yells back, pulling the blanket over the rest of his head.

The three of us go into the basement and I undress Calvin, lifting him into a large metal utility sink. We leave his clothes in a pile by the staircase and Zoe says we will have to burn them or throw them away. She unpacks the paper bag and first we wash Calvin hard, with syrupy tar shampoo. Then she pulls out two disposable douches and begins squeezing them onto Calvin.

"It works," she says, sensing my trepidation. "The vinegar solution helps kill the smell."

"Makes sense."

Before we put Calvin to bed, I spray deodorant on his sheets to drown any remaining scent of skunk.

There is a bowl of Granny Smith apples on the kitchen table and Zoe slices one into sections, taking a slab of cheddar cheese from the refrigerator and cutting it into separate pieces as well. The two of us sit on the floor, in the living room, eating apple and cheese and drinking Budweiser.

"Where's your wife?" Zoe asks, rather suddenly—unexpectedly.

"Now she's back in Texas, with her family."

"You stay in touch?"

"Not so much. A little, I guess. She called here the other day—mostly to talk to Calvin. Actually, she wants to come see him."

"Is she?—coming, I mean."

"I don't know yet. I haven't really decided."

"And it's up to you?"

"I suppose. We kinda have this unwritten code. Seeing as it was her that left, I get to call the shots—as far as Calvin's concerned."

"Hmm."

She pulls off her boots and crosses her legs, yoga-style.

"You don't agree with that?"

"It's not for me to say."

"I'm asking you to say."

"In that case," she says, taking the last sip of her beer, "then I don't think I agree. Obviously, I don't know your ex-wife, but she must have, at one time or another, been a decent person for you to have been attracted to her—for you to have married her. Maybe we selectively forget those things, those good things about somebody that made us love them, once the romance is gone. It makes it easier, I guess."

"She left him."

"You know why?"

"Really, I think it was that she was confused. She was too emotionally immature to be a wife, a mother. It wasn't her time."

There is still so much of Kate's life, my life, I do not yet understand. Namely, what caused her to wander in the first place? It was as if by magic: something lost between us that we'd never get back. Suddenly she felt differently about me, Calvin, us. "You're too hard on people," Kate once told me. It is a thing I have not forgotten. She repeated this proclamation the day before she left, arms crossed, indignant. "You're wrong," I said, because, really, it was all I *could* say. Please, not this: do not leave me alone, almost alone. There I stood, in the hallway, lamely clawing for words, trying to keep the discussion alive. And now, I confess, there are times when I hold tight to her belief—looking to accept blame. I want an explanation, even when there really isn't one to be had. Not one I can reach out and feel swimming between the swollen bellies of my fingers, like motor oil.

When Zoe comes back into the room, after she has returned the remaining portion of cheese to the refrigerator and placed the empty bottles in their box beneath the sink, she kneels down so close that her hair tickles the side of my face. She takes my head in her hands and pulls me toward her, kissing me gently, first on the chin and nose and then full on the lips. I can taste the beer and tart apple in her spit and there is the slight smell of cheese, and I'm not sure if it belongs to her breath or mine.

Once upstairs, we pause beside the bathroom, embracing in its doorway. Our stocking feet slide on the smooth tile floor, pulling us farther inside until we collide with the back wall. We drop down, not stopping until my butt cheeks hit the edge of the bathtub. Zoe straddles me and the two of us fall back into the tub, my calves hanging over its porcelain lip.

"You warm?" she asks, unbuttoning my shirt.

Two nights before Kate wandered into her private, emancipated life, she and I made love for the final time against an old player piano in our living room. The felt pads covering the hammers had long since worn through, so when we banged into the keys the even, hardened ends colliding with the strings made a clanking noise that echoed against the sagging wood, resembling the pitch of muffled doorbells. When we had finished and my arms were extended so they formed a V, pinning Kate awkwardly to the empty roller, she dropped her chin on my collarbone and whispered, "Try not to breathe." I could feel my penis getting soft, shriveling, shrinking back from the tangled yarn of her groin. Also, I could feel the sticky wetness of semen creeping down the inside of her thigh. Again she said, "Try not to breathe," and this time I did. It seemed like for a long time and my lungs began to shiver before I finally inhaled, taking the musty air from behind the back of her neck, the air that belonged to the piano. There is nothing especially significant about this memory, other than it being the last time we made love, the last time I made love.

Zoe is slow, removing my clothing before her own. When she undresses she stands, never taking her eyes off my naked body slumped in the tub.

"Just hold me first," she says, lying on top.

We are still until she decides it is time to move, kissing the wiry diamond of hair lifting from the crevice between my nipples. Immediately I can feel my erection push into her stomach and I try to slide to one side or the other, but there is no room.

"It's all right."

She reaches down and rubs the underside of my penis with the back of her hand. Then she grabs it full and begins pulling in long, gentle strokes. There are other things I try to think about: leaky basements, the cold-water spigot against the bottom of my foot, Halloween candy that will make Calvin sick. But nothing works and I come in a terrific burst, with semen shooting its way nearly to Zoe's armpit. For this I want to apologize, to explain to her it has been quite a while since I have been intimate with a woman. Instead, I close my eyes tight, snapping my head back and losing myself in the warm, tender closeness of someone else, someone who can make me feel this rush.

It does not take long for me to get hard again, and this time Zoe climbs over and places me inside her. She lays her palms flat against the tile wall above, bracing herself as she rocks in easy waves that begin and end at the hinge of her hips. We both make the same gravelly moans, starting in the parched well of our throats. It feels so good, so foreign, that after I come for the second time I beckon her to continue, guiding her with my fingertips grazing the roll of her rear end. Soon my fingers lose contact with her skin and I lie quiet, motionless, as she retreats from the tub and walks to the sink. Neither of us speaks and after a few moments she hands me a cigarette from my coat pocket. She sits on the toilet beside me, the tinkling of her urine the only sound as we share the cigarette, alternately blowing smoke into an open crack of window.

Then Zoe reaches down and taps me on the arm, gesturing with her head to the doorway. Calvin, standing in his turned-up pajama bottoms and floppy T-shirt, rubs the sleep from his eyes. He still smells of douche bags and skunk.

"Does her tummy hurt?" he asks, and I know exactly what he means. Sometimes, when Calvin has a stomachache or is constipated, I sit with him in the bathroom and hold his hand while he is on the toilet. When he was younger, a year or so ago, I would also read to him.

"Yeah," I say. "She isn't feeling so well. Too many sweets."

"Oh."

He takes out his stepladder and climbs to the sink for a glass of water. When he has finished he leaves without saying another word, without asking us why we are not dressed. Again there is silence and I close my eyes and reach for Zoe, rubbing small, perfect circles onto her knee.

NINE

Harper Blyth is leaning against the hood of my car, eating popcorn from a red-and-white striped cardboard box. His wife, Natalie, is seven months pregnant and she is standing to his side, her bloated belly pushing out from beneath the folds of a tan topcoat. When I approach, Natalie raises a mittened hand and waves.

"Sorry," she says.

After winning its first four games, the Tarent High basketball team has lost by nearly twenty points to Creekside. In the locker room, once the game had ended, I wanted to tell the boys not to get upset about this, not to let it ruin the rest of their weekend. Instead, I complained about their lack of full-court defense, about Russell Johns's repeated refusal to pass the ball to the open man, and about overall poor shot selection—particularly by Noah. Shortly after I left them and was walking down the corridor to the parking lot, I stopped briefly, debating whether or not I should go back and apologize. But then Jess Thomas, the principal and scoreboard operator, came over to console me and the two of us left the building together.

"This was not the game to come to, huh?" says Harper.

"No," I say, kissing Natalie on the cheek. "It was not."

They invite me for coffee, but I decline, saying that Zoe is babysitting Calvin and she deserves to be relieved of those duties.

"You're spending a lot of time with her," says Harper, sarcastically wagging his eyebrows.

"Leave him be," says Natalie. She plants an elbow in his ribs and then reaches for his hand, leading him toward their car, which is parked bumper-to-bumper with mine. Harper is a good husband, helping Natalie into the passenger seat. He spits onto his thumb and wipes the corner of her mouth. "Mustard," he says, before easing the door closed and walking around to the other side.

Standing erect, I must appear gloomy, because as Harper backs out he rolls down his window and smiles. "Things are not so bad," he says. Then, as he pulls away, he shouts, "Eat a burrito!"

Near the end of our first year of law school, after Harper had split with his then girlfriend and was so depressed he insisted he was going to drop out and sell seashell-sculptured trinkets on the beaches of Spain, George Redwin and I took him to a Mexican restaurant at 1:30 in the morning and made him eat four burritos. We told him he would feel better afterwards. Of course, he did not. He became ill on the walk home, spraying the steps of the student union with vomit that came in salsa-speckled splashes. It took all of George's and my powers of persuasion to convince two campus police officers that Harper was not intoxicated, only sick from heartbreak and fierce Mexican cooking. From that night on, whenever our minds became encumbered with thoughts so debilitating that we were incapable of studying, watching television, shooting pool, etc., we would escape for burritos.

At home, Calvin has fallen asleep in my bed with the radio turned low and his loose crayons scattered across the cotton sheets. His tiny breaths cause the mattress to twitch, leading some of the crayons to roll into the crack underneath the headboard.

"He was tired," says Zoe.

She is reading a textbook in the gauzy, funnel-shaped light of a desk lamp. The pages of her book hold pink fluorescent dashes from a marker she has in her right hand.

"We lost."

She slips the book into a leather satchel and then rises, coming to my side and kissing my neck.

"This is not such a good night for you, huh?" She removes her coat from the back of a chair. Then, without looking up, she says, "I spoke to Kate."

"What do you mean?"

"She called here."

"What did she say? What did *you* say?"

"Nothing much. She sounded surprised that I answered, that a woman answered." Zoe zips her coat and the two of us walk downstairs, into the front hallway, beside the door. "She wants to come here."

Who the fuck is she, I wonder, to talk about such things with Zoe. Or does she have to crowbar her way into this relationship, too?

"What else?" I ask.

"She wants to come next week."

"Next week? *Not* next week. Next week is too soon."

"Too soon for what?"

"Just too soon."

As she unfastens her keys from a clip inside her bag, I ask her if there was anything else. Really, what I want to know is why Zoe does not seem angrier, teeming with jealousy.

"She wanted to sing to Calvin. Something from when he was a baby."

"Did you let her?"

She nods and then slips her arms through mine, hugging me so that her wrists tug gently against my spine. In the hanging wall mirror I watch my eyes widen. Also, I can see the elastic waistband of her coat has caught on her hip, curling beneath itself.

"What are you gonna do?" she asks.

"I need to sit with this for a while."

"You don't have a while."

Perched in the doorway, I watch Zoe walk to her truck. Before she climbs in, she knocks on the windshield, for no apparent reason, and says, "She seems sweet, Gordon."

Mostly she was sweet, I think, climbing the stairs

to the house. Except for those times when she was not.

"What would you do?" I call out, peering over my shoulder.

"Hmm," Zoe says. "I'm not the right person to ask."

"Why?"

She sighs, loud. Brushing the bridge of her nose, she says, "Do you know Bailey Foss?"

"From down at the paper? He's an editor or something?"

"Or something."

"And?" I turn to face Zoe, squarely. Now she is tapping at the open pickup door with the toe of her boot.

"I dated him for almost a year."

"Really?"

"Yep."

"*Really?*"

"You want him paying me social calls?"

I smile, hooking my thumbs through the belt loops on my pants. "You two got any kids?"

"None that I know of."

"The thing is—"

"Look, it must be hard for her, too—being away from Calvin for so long, being away from you. I can appreciate that. Really, I can." She reaches forward, lifting something from the vent in the dashboard—yarn or a twisted piece of wire, it's too dark to tell. "I just don't want to stand around and watch."

"Watch what?"

"Whatever."

I walk back down the steps and rest my elbow

against the roof of the truck, staring at Zoe beneath the curve of my armpit.

"We are *very* divorced," I say.

Zoe nods and after a few minutes of silence dense like a soggy sponge, she tells me she has to get home.

"You okay with this?" I ask.

She shrugs.

"Come on. Be okay with it. For me."

"Why can't I not be okay with it? For me."

I reach through the parted window and her skin feels cold as sheet metal.

"Think about what you want from me, Gordon. What you want from us."

"It's just that this is a hard time."

She adjusts a knob beside the steering wheel. "It will always be a hard time, for one reason or another."

"Not always. Not if Kate doesn't come."

"Go to bed," she says, starting her truck.

She pulls away swiftly and in the evening air I kick pebbles until they ring against the copper pipes below the porch.

Calvin likes to count rocket ships on long car trips. He presses his face flat against the window and scans the vast, fretless prairie for silos, which he calls rockets. "There are twins," he will announce after seeing two bound together by brass piping. Because he often loses track of the numbers when he gets past twenty, it is really my responsibility to keep count. Today, from the right side of the car, he has spied thirty-one from Tarent to Lawrence.

"There musta been more than that," he says when I sound the total.

"No," I answer, patting him on the thigh. "Not unless you missed a few."

In the long, fragile months after Kate left, I used to take Calvin to the parking lot of the building she lived in when the two of us first met, and lay him across my stomach and lap. There I would rock him gently to sleep while Brahms played on the cassette deck of the car. He did not know where we were, of course, but I would stare up at her old window and watch as someone else, someone other than Kate, passed behind the illuminated glass.

Because her time with Calvin was so brief, so frighteningly nondescript, I always find it difficult knowing the best way to refer to her. Sometimes I call her Mom, other times simply Kate. Today I call her both.

"Last night Mom sang to you?"

He nods, his eyes busy trying to focus on the rapid-passing scenery of downtown Lawrence.

"What did Kate sing? Do you remember?"

First he says no, he does not remember. But I press him.

"It was the sun song. Somethin' about the sun."

For some reason, shortly after Calvin turned one, the only song he allowed Kate and me to play on the stereo or sing to him was the Beatles' "Here Comes the Sun."

"You like that song," I tell him.

He shrugs and then says, "Her voice isn't so good."

We both smile.

In the library at the University of Kansas, Calvin leafs through a book filled with large, glossy photographs of wild animals. He points at pictures and then softly, to himself, tries to mimic the noises the various animals make. After he lets out a snorting sound, I look up and ask him what it was.

"This." He is tapping a flamingo.

"You think that's how it sounds?"

"Maybe," he says and turns the page.

We take a break after an hour or so, sitting on a wooden bench in the front corridor of the library, drinking apple juice. Calvin does not eat any crackers, he only wants to hold the plastic mug that screws on the top of the thermos.

"Careful," I say, placing both his hands around the cup.

He leans over and begins lapping at the juice like a dog or a cat.

"There's something I want to talk to you about," I say. He is not listening, busy instead making gurgling noises.

"It was the *sun* song," he says, sounding slightly perturbed. "I already told you."

"Yeah, I know." I take the cup from him and pour the remaining finger of juice into a sand-filled ashtray. The juice pools briefly before it is absorbed. "It's not about that. It's about something else."

Now he reaches for a sliced pear I have wrapped in a sandwich bag.

"Wait a minute," I say, turning him so that we are facing each other. "We're going to talk first, okay?"

When he is still for a moment, I start. "This is about Kate, your mom, coming to visit us here."

"In Kansas," he states, confidently.

"Right. In Kansas." I screw the cup back onto the thermos and ease my hands into a clasp, above my belt. "She wants to see us—I mean, you. Mostly you. It's been awhile, almost two years, and I wanted to know how you felt about her coming here, to our home."

"Is she gonna bring me anything?"

This is what matters to a small boy; his needs are immediate. Motherless, half orphaned, he knows of no other way of life. Really, what he wants most is not a mother but a bulldozer with a crane attached to its rear, the kind of crane that has a dangling, braided chain that allows a boy to yank open and closed the toothy shovel at its end.

"That's not what's important, Cal. What matters, what *really* matters, is that she wants to come be with you."

"For how long?"

"I'm not sure. Maybe a few days—a week."

His legs are short and do not reach the ground, so when he leans back, his feet stick straight up toward the ceiling.

"I like Zoe."

"I like her, too. She's not going anywhere; it's just that Kate—your mother—is going to be around for a few days also."

Still, he does not fully understand what this means and, truthfully, neither do I. He watches as a girl drops change into a soda machine and he blinks big when her can of Diet Coke makes a thunk as it hits bottom. When he turns back to me I remove Kate's postcard of the Bali lizard from my shirt pocket.

"She sent you this."

"Oooh. It's a dinosaur."

"No, it's a lizard. They're only about this size," I say, holding my thumb and forefinger several inches apart.

"Lizard," he repeats. "Does she have lizards?"

"No. But she took a trip far away, to Bali, and they had lizards there."

"She coulda brought some back."

"She didn't. But she did send you the postcard. That was nice."

He holds the postcard close to his face, lizard to lips. "I guess she could come," he says.

Later, as I sit alone at the kitchen table drinking three muddy cups of decaf in a row, this vision is what finally allows my stubbornness to crumble and chance letting Kate back in: it is the image of Calvin's breath warming the postcard that causes me to remember something small, something nearly insignificant about Kate. Once, when we were all together, Calvin had crawled into a laundry closet and ripped open a large box of washing-machine detergent. We found him sprinkled white, spitting powder in clumps on his little hands. Quickly, Kate ran and got her camera, taking several pictures of Calvin before cleaning him off. In the months to follow, I would occasionally catch her staring at one of these photographs, holding it up close to her mouth, as Calvin did with the postcard. I don't know why she did this, because, after all, she had the real Calvin in the next room. Perhaps she simply wanted to be reminded of another time, of an instant, a moment when she was happy and anything, everything was still possible.

When I pull into the driveway, after basketball practice, the house is shrouded in a damp, wispy mist. Calvin is chasing Argos around the yard while Zoe sits on the porch, watching. She is wearing a black-and-red-plaid jacket zipped to her neck, and as she stands to greet me, Moonie darts out from behind the swing. Zoe takes my hand, stroking it briefly before kissing me on the wrist. Today, her brother got into a fistfight at school and was required to sit in study hall for most of the afternoon. I do not tell her this, though.

"There is something for you and Calvin in the freezer," she says. "It came a few minutes ago."

"What do you mean, *it came*?"

"Delivery. I had to sign for it."

Calvin knows about the package and he follows me into the kitchen, asking if he should get the scissors.

"This is what we do," I say, looking at Zoe. "Work, play, and open packages from my mother."

Inside the cardboard box, stenciled on all sides with the words *Refrigerate immediately*, is a Styrofoam cooler packed with dry ice and two cartons of automobile-shaped Popsicles.

"The middle of November," I say. "People in Kansas do not eat Popsicles in the middle of November."

Calvin's hand is outstretched and I give him one, placing the rest back in the freezer.

"Before dinner?" Zoe asks.

I wave her off.

"It's mushy," says Calvin. He takes a bite and his purple Pontiac slides from the stick onto the floor. Instantly, Argos tramps over and licks it up. Calvin tries to push him away, but is not strong enough.

"He's eating my pop," he says, shaking his arms. "*Ahh*, my pop!"

"That's all right, it wasn't frozen enough. We'll wait until after dinner when the rest have had a chance to get harder."

I am convinced Calvin is going to complain, but he does not. He simply walks into the other room, jacket hanging from his waist like a furry tail.

"Tomorrow I'm going to Oklahoma," says Zoe, lifting a dish of chicken parts that have been soaking in the sink. "A group of us are spending a few days on this guy's ranch studying his cattle. It's for a lab."

"No ranches around here?"

"His livestock is diseased. We're going with one of the professors."

"What's wrong with them?"

"Don't know."

Lying in the darkness, after Calvin has been put to sleep, Zoe asks me to tell her something good.

"What do you mean?"

"I don't know, just tell me something good."

"Let's see," I say, rubbing the stubble on my chin.

"Well, Joyce and Rob Ives made their first payment to Gooland's. This morning they walked in together and laid a check right down next to the register."

"No, not like that. Something *good.*"

Argos ambles into the doorway and pauses before dropping in a heap beside the closet.

"How about this: my roommate in college used to put ketchup on his spaghetti when we'd run out of tomato sauce."

"Yuck."

"Yeah, yuck. So, is that good?"

"It wasn't what I was hoping for—but it's good."

"What were you hoping for?"

"I don't know."

"Why don't *you* tell *me* something good."

She combs her fingers through the shaggy hair that has spilled onto her forehead.

"Okay." She exhales with force, so that near the end, just as she is about to curl her lips to speak, she lets out a short whistle. "This afternoon, while you were at work or basketball, Calvin and Meg were standing over on the end of the porch holding on to the railing, up near their heads. Really, I almost walked right past them until I noticed that both their pants were pulled down to their knees. Calvin was pissing over the side, into the flower beds. Meg was watching, and after a minute or two, she turned to him and said, 'Well, you can't do this,' and she reached down and removed a nickel from her vagina."

"*Nooo.*"

"Yep."

"What'd you say?"

"Nothing. Absolutely nothing."

Turning on my back, I let out a chuckle and then say, "You're right, that's good."

Deep into the night, with Zoe sleeping soundly, I turn on the light so I can write the incident down on a piece of notepaper on the bedstand. This is something I want to remember, something I want to tell Calvin about when he is old enough to understand.

Once there is stillness again, it occurs to me how nice it feels to share stories with someone in bed. How pleasant it is to hear someone else breathing, to hear the unique rasp of Zoe's breath as it drags through the tunnel of her windpipe and nose. With my vision still adjusting to the darkness, I stare at her bare shoulders until my eyes can tell the difference between her freckles and the burning, black splotches of light against my pupils.

From where I am lying in bed, facing the doorway, I can see the back of Zoe's body as she leans over the sink in the bathroom to wash her hair. She has just finished and she twists her damp locks into a towel and then wraps the towel turban-like above her head. When she comes back into the bedroom she is quiet, careful, thinking I am still asleep. She slips on one of my sweatshirts, her blue jeans, and then sits down beside the window to pull on her boots.

"When are you coming back?" I ask.

"I didn't know you were awake."

"Mmm."

"It should only take a few days—maybe Saturday or Sunday. We'll have to go back again, though."

Sitting up, I realize how little I know about what interests Zoe, about her classes, her work. It is not because I do not care, but rather because I have not had the time to care. While I was hacking out a breathing hole from beneath my studies at law school, Kate showed patience, too.

"Are you excited about this? About going?"

First, she shrugs and then, before reaching for her coat, she says, "No one wants to see animals suffer, to see them suffer and die."

When she comes to the side of the bed and kisses me, I can taste toothpaste on her lips.

"Gordon," she says, removing the towel from her head and draping it flat over the back of a chair. "I want you to do something for me."

"Anything."

"I'm taking the truck. I'm not sure, but Noah may need a ride home from practice today or tomorrow. Will you give him one?"

"Don't you think he'd rather have one of the other players take him?"

"Probably, but I'd like it if you'd ask him—just in case."

I nod.

There is nothing else and I stay in bed for some time, listening to Zoe speaking to Calvin downstairs, and then the sounds of her leaving: the slamming of the screen door, her footsteps in the loose stones of the driveway, the starting of her truck, and finally the cool, quiet of silence. Closing my eyes, I think of doing something nice for her, taking her away, only the two of us, leaving Calvin at Charlotte's house for a few days. Perhaps someplace warm where we can watch our white, doughy skin turn the color of cinnamon.

TEN

About three miles or so north of the Tarent city limits, beyond a low-hanging concrete overpass leading to the Interstate, is a narrow, poorly kept stretch of road that serves as the driveway to Noah's girlfriend's house. For a while there is nothing but night, broken only by the faded yellow of my headlights. Finally, suddenly, we pull around a short, sharp corner and can see the glowing twin orbs of streetlamps. After we straighten out, Noah points into the windshield at a figure standing beside a rusted, stone-colored tractor.

"That's Ann," he says.

She takes a long, smoky drag from a cigarette and then taps off the ashes into the top of a soda can. Noah pauses for a moment before getting out of the car, and I'm not sure if it's because he wants to say something. He does not, only closing the door lightly behind. Before I back out I roll down the window, halfway, and ask, "It's okay for you to be here?"

They glance at each other and then Noah nods. Of

course, I know he's lying, but I leave them alone. It is difficult to grow up with only one parent, I tell myself, switching on the brights for the drive back into town. "Some people have not had it so easy," I remember my mother saying to me when I was younger as she packed up used clothing and flatware for the Salvation Army. "We need to give them every advantage we can." Then who will provide living utensils, worn with age, for Calvin? I wonder. Where will they come from? Who will know that he has not had it so easy?

Today the air feels warmer and Calvin is sitting on the back stairs dressed only in jeans and a cotton sweater. In between bites, he pushes his Ferrari Popsicle precariously close to the ground, leaving behind a green juice trail of exhaust. He is making a motoring sound with his tongue. This morning Zoe returned, bringing with her red-and-white Oklahoma Sooner baseball caps for Calvin and me. I'm wearing my cap backwards, catcher-style, while Calvin carries his by its adjustable strap, like a purse. Rocking in the swing, I do the Sunday crossword puzzle, occasionally looking up at Zoe, who is repairing the muffler on her truck. The telephone sounds and I wait for three rings before rising to answer it. At first there is silence on the other end, but just before I prepare to hang up, Kate speaks.

"Gordon? I wasn't sure if I dialed the right number. It didn't sound like you."

"It's me."

"Well"—she makes noises as if she is unwrapping something, cellophane. "I'm here."

The other day, before I picked Calvin up from Charlotte's house, I called Kate and told her it was all right to come, although I did not expect her to arrive so quickly.

"Where are you staying?"

"Amis Motor Lodge. Do you know where that is?"

She is in the southeast section of town, near the high school, not ten minutes from our house.

"Yes," I say.

"I flew into Lawrence and rented a car. The drive was easy, like the man at the Hertz counter said it would be."

"Uh-huh."

"So . . . well." She pauses, and then, "What should I do?"

The directions are simple, but I let her repeat them, to be safe. She wants to take a quick shower, clean up from the trip, and then she'll come over. She waits, taking a breath before telling me she is excited, excited to see us both.

Outside, Calvin has finished his Popsicle and is now using its stick to dig a trough in the moist earth. Lying on her back, Zoe asks me to kick her an allen wrench. From above, only her legs are left unobscured, mysteriously twitching from beneath the truck's corrugated metal bed.

"It was Kate," I say, talking to Zoe's boots.

"What was Kate?"

"On the phone. It was Kate. She's here."

"Where?"

"Here. In Tarent. She's staying at Amis Motor Lodge."

"I didn't even know you told her she could come," says Zoe, reaching blindly for a roll of copper wire.

"Yeah," I say, running my hands along the smooth steel siding of the truck. "I told her while you were away."

"She sure got here fast."

I nod, but Zoe cannot see me. Some time passes and then she slides out from underneath. She stands and brushes the dirt from her ass and the backs of her thighs and calves.

"C'mon, Argos," she says, opening the door on the passenger side of the truck and patting the seat.

"Where're you going?"

"Home."

"Why?"

"I shouldn't be here when Kate arrives. Besides, you three need some time alone."

"No," I say, grabbing her around the waist and pulling her close. "I want you here. I *need* you here."

"No you don't," she says, kissing me on the tip of my nose. She walks around to the other side of the truck, waving goodbye to Calvin before climbing in. "You'll do fine," she says through the glass. "Be nice."

Then it is only Calvin and me, alone behind the house, waiting for the arrival of his mother. There is so much I had wanted to say to prepare him, but instead I choose only silence. We build a small fort using twigs and stones and then I take him inside and wash the sticky green Popsicle from his face and hands.

She is driving a white Ford Taurus and I watch her from my upstairs window. She sits still for some time, long enough to check her face twice in the rearview mirror and look into a large brown purse at her side. Calvin yells out that someone is here, someone is in the driveway.

I call him to the stairwell. "It's your mother," I say, tucking in the front of his sweater. He pulls back, complaining he doesn't like it that way. "Listen, keep it in for me."

He huffs and the two of us walk to the front door. He looks surprised, because normally we use the back entrance. But normally his mother does not come to visit.

"Hello," she says, clinging briefly to the door handle of her car before walking up the pathway.

"Say hello," I whisper to Calvin. He does not seem terribly thrilled by Kate's arrival until he sees that she is carrying a dictionary-sized package beneath her arm.

"Is that mine?" he asks.

Kate smiles and nods. In two years she has not changed much physically. Her hair is lighter, blonder, and her skin is dark from sun. A small silver cross hangs from her left earlobe and she has a pair of tortoiseshell sunglasses clipped through an open buttonhole of her denim shirt. She is wearing no makeup, save a gentle rub of lipstick the shade of blood oranges. The hollows of her cheeks seem deeper, slightly. Leaning down, she will not surrender the package until Calvin gives her a hug. She lets out a moan, from her diaphragm, and then wraps her arms around Calvin's back, dropping her chin over his shoulder. Calvin seems to know this is important and he does not struggle, as he does with his grandmother or strangers, or sometimes even with me. Kate runs her fingers up his spine and neck and through the feathery ends of his hair. When she turns her face to breathe, like a swimmer, I can see she is crying. Slowly, she releases him, blotting her wet cheeks with the heel of her hand.

"Okay, now enough of this," she says, reaching for the box at her side. "I didn't really know what to get."

Hurriedly, Calvin scratches through the wrapping paper to reveal a miniature DC-10 airplane.

"The batteries are supposed to be inside."

Calvin peels back the ends of the box, pulls free his aircraft, and accidently flips the switch that turns a set of red wing lights blinking.

"Enamored," I say, watching him clutch the flashing toy against his chest.

"Really, I had no idea what to get him. I mean, little boys are so hard to shop for."

I nod, walking onto the grassy hump of soil that is our front yard. Kate starts to follow, then stops midway, between Calvin and me, as if waiting for an invitation. Turning to face the two of them, to face the house, I raise my arms as if nailed to a crucifix, opening one palm and gesturing upwards, outwards.

"This is our life," I announce. "This is how we live."

Mostly, Kate spends the evening observing Calvin: watching him run his new airplane across the floor, eating half a bowl of alphabet noodle soup or a piece of bread smeared with strawberry preserves. These are things she has not seen him do, things he was almost too young to do alone before she left. When he puts on his pajamas, she reaches over and rubs his round belly, seemingly fascinated by its gummy, resilient texture. She sits on the edge of his bed and tells him about her trip to Bali, about how people had to watch the ground while walking, otherwise they were bound to step right on a lizard—squishing it. Finally, she tells him how she would wheel him in a shaded carriage to a park in Ann Arbor when he was a baby and talk to him, just like she's talking to him now. Before we turn out the lights, she kisses him on his forehead, cheek, and then hard on his neck.

"I had nearly forgotten how sweet he is," she says in the hallway.

We sit at the kitchen table and I pour out two glasses of Scotch, with lots of ice, the way Kate likes it. She rolls the tumbler quickly between the palms of her hands, beads of perspiration flicking from the glass, catching the light like dust motes.

"You look well," she says, between sips.

"This place agrees with me."

"It's not too small?"

I shake my head and walk over to the sink, running some cold water into my glass.

"You and Harper getting along all right?"

"Sure. Work's fine. Quiet."

"Not much need for the great litigator out here, huh?"

"Things change," I say, stirring my drink with one of Calvin's abandoned Popsicle sticks. "You never know how life's going to jump up, fuck with you."

"Like maybe a wife leaving."

"Or a mother," I say, turning to peer out the window at her clean white car in the drive.

"Or a mother."

Walking to the table, I spin a chair and straddle it, backwards, laying my forearms across the top of the headrest.

"How's your life?" I ask, looking directly into the almond-hued irises of her eyes.

"Different. Different than when you knew me." She stops to take another drink. "I've seen a lot—been so many places I never knew, never even imagined existed. Bali, Zanzibar, Beijing, Toledo—"

"Ohio?" I ask, smirking.

"Spain. Toledo, Spain," she says, missing my attempt at sarcasm. "That's education. Semesters, summers—whole years abroad should be required curriculum at all colleges."

She quiets, suddenly, fingering a torn page from one of Calvin's coloring books. It is a picture of a baker holding a tray of freshly made cakes, pies, and sticky buns. Calvin has crayoned the confections mostly orange and pink.

"Last March we drove to St. Louis," I say.

Kate smiles, uncomfortably. She is another person, someone I no longer truly know.

At our wedding reception, index cards were left at the place setting of every guest. Printed across the top of each card was the inscription, "Advice for the newlyweds . . ." Most of the responses were humorous, and we read them all later in bed on our honeymoon. Not so long afterwards, when I was packing for Calvin and my move to Kansas, I found the cards, hairy with mildew, stored in a shoe box. All the answers are right here, I thought, simply for the asking. You, too, could solve each and every marital problem by rifling through these index cards, searching for the proper advice—the cure for whatever ails you. One I remember, even now, ended with the phrase: "Don't lose the connection. It is special, it is rare."

But something inflated between us, quickly, and would not burst.

"Thank you for letting me come," she says, smoothing out the wrinkled coloring-book page against the hard surface of the table. "It means the world to me."

Beside the closet in the front hallway we discuss plans to meet tomorrow morning for brunch. I hold open Kate's coat and she slides her arms through. She asks if she can keep the colored page, and when I say yes, she neatly folds it into four sections and places it inside her purse. Staring down at the muddied tips of her shoes, she manages, "I'm sorry."

"For what?"

"For things. That our lives became so separate. That things turned out so different than we planned. And"—slowly, she nudges wider a crack between the front door and the molding, and from where I am standing, behind,

I can see her lower lip tremble—"that I have not been there every evening to kiss Calvin good night."

Nothing is easy about Kate trying to bleed her way back into Calvin's life, back into our lives. We hug awkwardly, rapidly, and then she drives back to her motel room, alone, with me on the front step in my stocking feet.

Cigarette smoke filters through a vent in the Tarent High locker room and Noah is standing on a chair, waving the smoke toward his face before inhaling deeply. He has not seen me enter, but I throw a broken piece of chalk at his hip to call his attention. They have won, again, and are wandering about the small, cement room dressed in towels and boxer shorts. Midway through the third quarter, after Eric Shaw sank a jump shot to put the Trojans ahead by 19, I realized that I had very little to do with the success of this team. It is a talented collection of athletes and the best thing I can do is offer some well-timed advice and then stand back and enjoy.

"You played a good game," I say, handing a Kleenex to Chris Rayles, who is rather vigorously picking at his right nostril. "Practice, tomorrow, usual time." Before I leave them, I ask, "Would someone please do me a favor? Last person out tonight flip the lock on the double doors."

Calvin and Kate have spent the day together and are waiting for me in the front lobby. This is the first home game Zoe has missed, but we are meeting her at Cale's for a quick bite once her shift has ended. When I arrive, Calvin is speaking rather emphatically to an older gentleman in a maroon jacket, explaining the two switches on his airplane: one to operate the lights and the other, the engine noises.

"And do you have any idea how fast this type of jet travels?"

"Not really," says Calvin, rubbing the nose cone with his thumb. "But it's fast. Faster than my dad's car."

This causes both Kate and the older man to laugh.

"Faster than my car?" I ask.

"Prob'lee."

"Okay, then," I say, lifting the bangs from his eyebrows.

At Cale's we take a table in the rear, beside an unplugged Addams Family pinball machine and a slanted painting of two fishermen hauling in a net at high sea. Calvin kneels on a chair and waves his airplane across the room at Zoe. For several minutes we are still, listening to the jukebox rumble from one twangy country song to the next. Some men would not put Zoe, or themselves, in this situation. Thorny, hazardous. But now I am selfish. More than anything, I need her support. And Kate will not show spite; she will mind her tongue. She is grateful, I know, that I have allowed her into our lives again, however short the visit.

Finally, Kate opens a menu and says, "She's very pretty." As if staged, called, Zoe carries over a cork-lined tray with three bottles of Budweiser, placing them in front of Kate, Calvin, and me.

"You let him drink beer?" asks Kate.

"It's orange juice," says Zoe. "He likes it in these bottles."

Then Zoe drops the tray to her side and reaches for Kate's hand. "Hi, I'm Zoe."

Kate introduces herself, too, and I apologize for my lapse in manners.

"We're used to that by now," says Zoe, winking at Kate and Calvin. "You'll have to excuse me for a few minutes. Just need to total my receipts and then I'll be finished."

She cannot take long enough. If I were standing on the outside, peering inward, I would give this whole little scene a gentle bump, like someone trying to keep a spinning silver ball from dropping between the flippers on that Addams Family pinball machine. Watching Zoe and Kate together in the same state, in the same *room*, leaves me short of breath. I make eye contact only with Calvin and some old guy sitting at the table behind us.

After fried-chicken baskets all around, we drink coffee and Kate tells Zoe about her uncle's ranch in north Texas, near the Oklahoma border town Zoe recently visited. At one point during their conversation, Zoe removes a small notepad from her purse and writes down something Kate says about a blue peeling around some of the cattle's noses. When their discussion aimlessly wanders to Calvin, who is nearly asleep, his head resting against my thigh, I mention that perhaps we should get him home.

She has not seen her son in half a lifetime, his lifetime, and we spend the evening discussing diseased bovines.

"Oh, it is late," says Kate.

Zoe maps out directions on the back of a napkin

from the parking lot of Cale's to Kate's motel. She does this without Kate's asking.

"Thanks."

"Here's the only tricky part," says Zoe, pointing to the black webbing of lines. "At this second stoplight, take the soft, angling right—not the hard one."

Beside the cars, Kate kisses Calvin and thanks Zoe and me for being so kind. Again, we make plans to meet tomorrow, sometime in the late morning. Then she leaves and Zoe follows me home in her truck.

"You don't say much to her," says Zoe, shirtless in bed.

"I don't know what I'm supposed to say."

"You're not *supposed* to say anything. But it looks so difficult for you—like you're really struggling."

"I am."

"With what?"

"I'm struggling not to explode. Not to start screaming at her—go absolutely nuts."

"Why?"

"What do you mean, why?" I ask, laying my book on the nightstand. "The real question is why haven't I done it yet. Why haven't I ripped her a new asshole for leaving—for leaving Calvin."

"Gordon," she says, sitting up, bracing herself against the headboard. "If you feel a need to do this, then do it. But you've got to have it out with her, tell her what's upsetting you. Not for her sake, but for yours." Zoe's breasts hang free, nipples rimmed in random Braille, shaking as she speaks. "Maybe this isn't only about Kate trying to make her peace with Calvin, but about you making peace with her. Christ, make peace with yourself."

"Peace, always peace. Maybe I don't want peace."

"Shut up, Gordon," she says, switching off the light above her side of the bed. "Act like a man."

The house shifts, settling ever so slightly into its brick base, and the walls respond with a creaky gasp.

"Weaverbirds," I say, into the black night air.

"Huh?"

"Weaverbirds. Do you know about them?"

"No, Gordon, I sure don't."

"They're indigenous to Africa—south of the Sahara, mostly. The male weavers build these enormous communal nests in the tops of trees or, sometimes, even telephone poles, using twigs and bark pieces and loose blades of grass. Then, as a way of courting, the males offer their nests to available females by hanging beak-down and flapping their yellow-and-green wings from the nests' short entry tubes. Often, the males fall and have to fly up again into the mouths of the nest."

Zoe crosses her ankles beneath our quilt, puffy with eiderdown.

"If the males fail to attract a female, they destroy their section of the nest and move on, hoping next time they will be more successful."

The bed dips as Zoe scoots closer to the middle, her hand groping for mine.

"And you're flapping your wings again," she says. "I can almost feel the breeze." She swallows, laboriously.

"If things don't work here, will you wreck this nest and move on?"

It is nearly two in the morning when the telephone rings and I lift it, instinctively, placing the receiver to my ear, saying nothing, simply letting my breath run across the perforated well of the mouthpiece. It is Sergeant Ray Lockwood of the Tarent Police Department and from what I can make out, in my semiconscious state, he is at the school with one of my basketball players. He wants me to come and take the boy home.

Standing at the foot of the bed, half dressed, I tell Zoe about school. "It shouldn't take long," I say. She responds with a grunt.

In the gymnasium, lit only by two emergency floodlamps above the door, Sergeant Lockwood is relaying information to someone on a hand-held walkie-talkie. Prone on the floor at his side is Noah, hands curled and cuffed and resting in the small of his back. There are six empty beer cans strewn atop a tattered army blanket.

"Is this really necessary?" I ask.

Sergeant Lockwood holds up his finger, signaling me to wait for a second. Then he says, "We can take the cuffs off now that you're here."

"What happened?"

"We were driving by, nightly patrol, and saw lights on in here. He broke in, was drinking beer with his girlfriend."

"I didn't break in," says Noah, speaking into the hardwood floor.

"He didn't break in," I add. "He was supposed to close up."

Sergeant Lockwood grabs Noah through his armpits and lifts him to his feet. Using a small silver key, he unlocks the cuffs and places them back into a holster on his belt. Noah stretches his arms, massaging the redness from his wrists.

"Where's the girl?" I ask.

"Her father came to get her about twenty minutes ago."

"Why didn't you call his father?"

"He asked us to call you."

When Sergeant Lockwood says this, Noah looks away, searching for something to hold in his line of vision, something in a direction other than mine. Before Sergeant Lockwood leaves, he tells me there aren't any charges, this time, but in the future I should call the police station if someone is going to be in the gym after midnight.

"He's underage too," says Sergeant Lockwood, kicking one of the beer cans on his way out.

The drive to Noah's house is nearly silent, the only noise being the gentle hiss of the car's tires against asphalt. Finally, as I stop at the end of his driveway so the headlights will not jump through the shutters and awaken his father, Noah turns to me.

"Listen—" he says, but before he can say anything else I slam my fist into the dashboard and he pulls back. Quiet.

"Cocksucker," I say, if only to hear how the word

sounds coming from my mouth. I want to strike him hard, in the face and neck and stomach, bringing blood that he will taste across the wide, fishy tail of his tongue. I want to hit him hard for all the times I've wanted to hit him, for the times I've wanted to hit my own son. But when I raise my arm, Noah doesn't flinch. He has been hit before. Maybe many times—at once and over scattered, passing years. He inhales, scared, the breath breaking into small, manageable pockets to be parceled sparingly along the honeycomb ridges of his lungs.

Above the radio, the clock snip, snip, snips along. Is this the kind of boy who later, once he is married and has a family of his own, watches the teenage girl next door undress from the bushes below her illuminated window? Or leaves his wife spooning strained peaches to their child so he can sleep with a waitress? Or, worst of all, decides one day that he has simply had enough?

"What are you going to do?" he asks.

This is a difficult question, and for the first time, maybe the first time ever, I hear genuine concern in Noah's voice. My father would have suspended him, immediately, and so, probably, would have Coach Miller. This is also what I want to do, once the need to abuse him physically passes. But before, in the gym, as Noah lay face down with those big, shiny handcuffs blazing in the floodlights and Sergeant Lockwood's oily boots not three feet from his head, all I could think about was Calvin and how maybe, someday, this might be him.

Some people have not had it so easy.

"I don't know," I say. "Why don't you get some sleep and we'll talk about it tomorrow."

He steps out of the car, slowly, holding the roof to steady himself. "Thanks," he says, so softly into his chest that for a moment I'm not sure if I imagined it. He said it, though, and then slammed the door, swiftly, to minimize the noise.

In the morning Zoe finds me sleeping on the couch, my overcoat pulled across my torso, my face poured into a crevice between two seat cushions. She is drinking milk from the carton, sitting on a ledge next to the fireplace, when I open my eyes.

"How come you're down here?"

"I was too tired to climb back upstairs. Besides," I start, removing some lint from my tongue, "I didn't want to wake you."

"That's sweet." She runs a finger along the straight edge of the carton, pulling loose a droplet of milk. She touches it to her lower lip and says, "It was Noah."

"What?"

"Last night, at school. It was Noah."

I nod, pulling the collar of my coat closer to my neck.

"Is he in trouble?"

"Mmm."

"Big trouble?"

"I don't know."

She brushes past on her way back to the kitchen, tapping me on the head with the milk carton.

"It was nice of you to get him."

I watch her standing over the kitchen sink, smoking a cigarette and thinking, about her brother, I presume.

Calvin walks in from behind, naked, holding his airplane beneath his right arm.

"Jesus," I say, rolling from my side onto my back. "Put on some clothes."

Zoe hands him a banana and he eats it in the doorway, facing me, his tiny penis winking with each bite.

"Why aren't you dressed?"

Still, he does not say anything; he is chewing, expressionless, as bewildered by me as I am by him. There is only the slappy, sucking sound of banana against inner cheek, like rubbers snapping loose from mud. When he is finished, Zoe stoops and whispers something into his ear and then he disappears.

"What'd you say?" I ask.

"I told him to get dressed."

"He listens to you." I feel lightheaded from sitting up too fast. "This is my life: an attorney stuck in the middle of—no, not an attorney: a marriage counselor in the middle of goddam Kansas whose son has taken to ignoring *him* and listening to his girlfriend . . ."

"So, now I'm your girlfriend?" asks Zoe, kneeling on the arm of the couch, smiling.

"Perhaps."

Once she leaves and I have showered and shaved, Calvin and I stop by the office before meeting Kate at Gooland's. When we arrive she is already drinking coffee and leafing through the local newspaper at a side table. Behind the register there is an open window into the kitchen area and Frankie Larch is staring out, at the dining room, a cigarette angled southward in the corner of his mouth. He nods when our eyes meet and then yells to me that Rob left his first payment the other day. Most of the front wall is repaired, except for some loose caulk seeping from underneath the windows and several exposed islands of cinderblock that will be hidden once the wooden panels are replaced.

"You look tired," says Kate, as I slide into the booth across from her.

Calvin is not very hungry, but I make him eat some oatmeal and part of my blueberry muffin. He wants to play in the fresh snow with Meg, before it melts or gets "smooshy." A man in blue coveralls is mixing plaster to spackle along the front wall, leveling the surface before they hang the paneling, and I tell Calvin he can go over and watch as long as he stands to the side and does not bother anyone.

"He's well behaved," says Kate.

"Most of the time."

She breaks off a corner of her muffin, bran, but does not eat it, instead flattening the loose crumbs with her index finger.

"When does he start school?"

"Next fall."

"And he'll go around here?"

I nod.

"The schools are okay?"

"They're fine."

The waitress comes over and pours us both more coffee, though my cup is half full.

"Well, I would imagine the classes are quite small. That's good."

"Uh-huh."

"Do you know any of the teachers? I mean, being that you're kind of like a member of the faculty—"

"It's totally different. The pre- and primary schools are at the opposite ends of town as the high school. I don't know any of those folks."

"Oh. I just—"

"Look, Kate, I appreciate your concern. But when the time comes, we'll handle it."

Using a paper napkin, she blots a spilled trail of coffee beneath her saucer.

"If you want me to apologize, I won't," she says, suddenly, sternly. "You know, Gordon, I'm not sorry I left. I had to. For me. I *am* sorry I've missed two years of Calvin's life, and I *am* sorry if I caused you pain, but I'm not sorry I left." She looks up, for the first time. "This isn't an easy thing for me, either, but I'm trying."

"I can forgive you for leaving me, Kate. But Calvin . . ."

"I'm not asking for your forgiveness. All I want is a chance to have a relationship with my son. And I can tell you this," she says, crossing her arms over her chest, "I *will* have that relationship, with or without your approval."

"Shit," I say, because I can think of nothing else besides spilling hot coffee down her lap.

The two of us do not say anything else until Calvin comes back, clutching something in his hand.

"What?" I ask, tapping his closed fist.

"He gave it to me," says Calvin, peering over his shoulder at the workman.

"Lemme see."

Calvin holds out his hand, revealing a wooden quarter-sized token with a buffalo painted on it. The token is good for one free drink at a bar in Wichita.

"It's a nice thing to have," I say, sliding it into the back pocket of Calvin's pants. "In case you're on the road or something."

Sometimes, when I'm alone, I will drive to a woodsy ridge about five miles from town and sit behind the wheel of my car, staring through the windshield at a narrow, twisted creek, watching the water split and reform as it collides with rocks and greasy bundles of sticks and leaves. Kate has taken Calvin and Meg to the movies for the afternoon. Earlier, at the office, Jess Thomas called me about last night. We have agreed to suspend Noah for two games, but I took much of the blame. From now on, I will be required to stay in the gym until the entire team has gone home.

The windows inside the car begin to cloud with moisture and when I turn, glancing across the passenger seat, I can see a crooked line of scrawl reappear above the door lock. At first, it does not seem like anything: the letters M and D, and maybe a Z. But upon closer examination, it may be that Calvin has written out the word Mom, as he did on the label of his man-o-war jar. Except for M, which for some reason he recognizes, the letters are only symbols to him; he can sing them but he doesn't really know how they fit together.

There are things he remembers about Kate, about her life with us before she departed, but he does not know he remembers them. They are simply passing thoughts in his little head, like the time he wanted to name his man-o-war Mom. He knows that Charlotte is Meg's mother and that my mother, Tish, lives in Florida and sends him funny packages. But he has never asked about Kate and why she does not live with us, in Kansas, or why she left in the first place. Someday, either Kate or I will explain this. In fact, Kate may decide to tell him in the car on the ride home from the movies with his fingers slick from butter and bright, gooey candy lodged in the craggy divots of his teeth.

Later, while I am breaking apart a head of iceberg lettuce into a worn, wooden bowl, Calvin sits on the counter with his airplane lying against his lap. He takes a loose piece of lettuce and holds it like a blindfold across the black glass of the cockpit, before sticking it into his mouth.

"In Texas they have horses," he says. "Lots of them."

"I know they do."

"Sometime, if we live there, I could have one."

"Well, it isn't likely we'll ever live in Texas."

He does not answer, instead reaching for my arm so that he can be lowered to the ground. Still, I do not know whether Kate told him the reasons she left us, but I'm quite certain she has promised him a horse. A large, bay colt of his own. In Texas.

After dinner I roam the living room, watering plants, while Zoe lies on the ground reading a textbook, her feet resting on the couch. She says this posture is good for her back, which aches from bending to shovel hay into the stalls where Willa is kept. She does not seem concerned that soon, Calvin, too, may have a horse.

"Oh, you don't know she said anything," says Zoe, scribbling something in the margin of one of her pages.

"Yeah, I do."

"And so what if she did. Big deal. You both know he's much too young."

"It's just the idea . . ."

She puts the book down at her side, leaving her pen between the binding to mark her place.

"You know how comfortable I am with this whole situation. It's not like I'm exactly thrilled having her hangin' around, either. But really, she's not awful."

"Fuck Kate!"

"Come on, Gordon. Stop."

"Fuck you, too!"

"I'm not even going to respond to that."

"Go ahead. Respond. Respond all the fuck you want."

The anger is so fiercely hot I can feel it fluttering behind my eyes. And then, from somewhere in my chest—deep near a place I despise knowing exists—I speak out Calvin's name in a sawed-off voice, a sing-songy high and low, like you might use to call a possum or raccoon before you bludgeon it with a sharpened ax handle. Hateful. Seething from low in my esophagus like before, like with Noah. "Fuck him," I mutter. In his little room, with no worries except what color his goddam horse is gonna be. Fuck him.

"Gordon, stop."

Only last week I found him burrowing beneath our living-room rug, crawling on all fours, with his back this movable hump, an enormous dust bunny—submerged. Again there was anger. "Maybe we're both dysfunctional," I thought. Taking a broomstick, I slapped at his tiny body twice, three times, before I heard him whimper.

Later, it was easy to make him forget: pizza, ice cream with sauce.

I bang the sprinkling can into the base of a floor lamp. Zoe slugs me in the ankle.

"This is not what I want," I say.

"It never is."

From her place on the ground she reaches up to make contact with my fingers, to make contact with me.

"You think Calvin understands all this?" she says. "Kate's just as confused. You know, the other day we spoke. Briefly." She fans out her hair against the rug. "It's more than her wanting to spend a few days with Calvin—or a few weeks even. She feels like you're dictating this little window of opportunity in which she can spend time with her son."

"What am I missing? Didn't she leave him behind and move on?"

"Not forever," says Zoe, stretching at the waist.

"And I suppose she gets to decide when forever is up."

"Do you know she's looking at property in the area?"

"Property to buy?"

"Yes, to buy."

"That's ridiculous." I sit in a wing chair, the empty

sprinkling can balanced on one knee. "That's fuckin' ridiculous."

"She doesn't hate *you*, Gordon."

I do not answer.

"You know something she told me? Something she remembered?"

Still, I am silent.

"It was about the funeral parlor, after your father died. She remembers taking you—practically forcing you to go to his casket. Then she told me she watched you from beside a set of lace curtains, alone."

This is a strange moment for Kate to recall. It was two or three days after my father died, and in the beginning I was afraid to see his corpse. Kate stayed with me in my bedroom at the house and it was she, ultimately, who convinced me to go and see the body. She had reminded me of something my father once said when I was a boy, something I repeated to her much later. He said, "Don't ever be afraid of nothin' that can't bite you." As she held my arm, gently massaging my right temple with her free hand, she assured me there wasn't anything at the funeral parlor that was going to bite me, least of all the lifeless body of my father.

At the parlor, she stood in the doorway as I walked to the side of his open casket. I wanted to touch him, to rub away some powder that had clotted in the dent on the side of his nose. But I didn't. Instead, I dropped to a knee and sang him his favorite song, from start to finish. It was a James Taylor song one of his players, Cooper Turo, used to sing accompanied by his guitar. Now I only remember the refrain: "So close your eyes/You can close your eyes it's all right/I don't know no love songs/And I can't sing the blues anymore/But I can sing this song/And you can sing this song/When I'm gone."

"It was a beautiful thing for her to choose to tell me," says Zoe. For a long moment, she seems lost in thought. "You've got to find a way to sort out your feelings."

I place my hands against the table, face-down, and say, "I've never had to share Calvin." Then I take a breath. "I'm not sure I know how."

"You'll do fine," she says, pushing her fist along the bumpy ridge of my knuckles. "And so will he."

We sit this way for some time, until, finally, Calvin shouts from upstairs. He has crashed his plane into the side of the television set and one of the lights has popped off. He wants me to come into the bedroom and help find it.

ELEVEN

Standing in the hallway at work beside the open door to Harper's office, I stare dumfounded as he rests naked on the couch, his arm flopped across the bridge of his nose, shielding his eyes from the early-morning sunlight. His legs are intertwined with the unclothed body of Joyce Ives. There is an empty fifth of bourbon on the desk, its weight smashing down on two Dixie cups. Before I can say anything, Calvin leaves my side and walks into the room. He bends, carefully, and from a distance peaks at the rigid lips of Joyce's vagina.

"I'm lookin' for money," he whispers, still a foot away.

As Joyce begins mumbling something, to herself, I yank Calvin back into the hall and tell him to wait for me in my office. This Harper hears, or thinks he hears, though for a moment he remains still, even settling deeper into the couch before, rapidly, sliding his arm away and gazing full-eyed into my face. Ever so briefly, he almost appears to smile. Then he scrambles to his feet, knocking Joyce onto the carpet as he gropes for his boxer shorts, which are dangling, rather neatly, from a desk lamp.

"Geez, Gordo, I didn't . . ." His voice gets lost somewhere in his throat as he searches for the rest of his clothing.

Crossing her ankles, Joyce doesn't seem bothered much by my intrusion. She lights a cigarette and adjusts herself on the floor, reaching beneath her bare ass to remove a used condom.

"I was sitting on this," she announces, holding it daintily above her head with two fingers.

Harper grabs the condom, along with the empty bourbon bottle and cups, and crams them into a trash can and then, after pausing to think for an instant, shoves them into his briefcase.

"This isn't what you think," he says.

"Yes it is," says Joyce.

"Well, it is"—shoeless, his shirt untucked and unbuttoned, he reaches down and pulls Joyce to her feet —"but it isn't."

"Hey," she says, as Harper holds open her jeans and tries to force one of her legs through.

"I'm going to leave you two alone," I say. "I'll be in my office."

"Really, you don't have to . . ."

Now Harper has Joyce hunched over his shoulder, still puffing a cigarette, as he fiddles with the buttons on her fly.

Calvin is perched behind my desk, so that from the entrance to the office, where I am, all I can see is his head. He is holding the Xeroxed copy of his hands that he made a couple months ago.

"This is me," he says.

"Yes, it is."

He lifts the paper to the window and tries to place one of his hands over the imprint. I'm not sure if he remembers how he made it, but before I'm able to ask, Harper pats me on the shoulder.

"I'm sorry about all this," he says.

"What the fuck are you doing?" I ask, pushing him into the hall, away from Calvin.

"I don't know. I mean, the first time—"

"First time? This wasn't the first time?"

He looks down and I don't know if it's because he is ashamed or because he wants to fasten his wrinkled necktie into a knot.

"Well?" I say, pressing him into the wall. "How long?"

"Maybe a year."

"A year? You two were fucking when you asked me to fleece her husband? Jesus, you're an asshole."

"We went to high school together. I've known her for years."

"That's great, Harp. That makes everything fine."

"I didn't say it made everything all right. I was just—"

"He was just saying sometimes these things happen," says Joyce, who emerges from Harper's office zipping the front of her coat.

"Like they just *happened* between Rob and that waitress?" I ask.

"No one wants it to happen with her husband."

"Get out of here, Joyce," I say. "Just get out."

Harper nods and she leaves through the rear entrance, milling about outside the glass door before getting into her car, Rob's car.

"Your wife is *pregnant*," I say, spitting out the sentence. "Christ."

"Don't you think—"

"No! Don't *you* think? Some part of you, some really fucked-up part, must have wanted this to come out—to get this discovered and over with. Why else would you have asked me to even come near her?"

As Harper is preparing to answer, Calvin wanders to my side.

"Baking bread," I announce, tipping my head to the heavens.

Both Calvin and Harper look at me, puzzled.

"They were baking bread, Cal," I tell him, because it's the only thing I can think to say. "And Harper, silly, crazy Harper, spilled flour all over their clothes and while they were waiting for the clothes to dry, well, the two of them fell asleep."

Calvin purses his lips, stepping back. He is too young, and he will believe whatever he's told.

"Bread," he repeats, retrieving a pen from the floor and walking again into my office, where, only yesterday, things were warm and safe. People remained fully dressed. Everything still made sense.

Harper stumbles, laying his forearm against the wall as he slips on his loafers. Now his life is truly without grace. Perhaps, in this moment, all things gentle and easy will end for Harper and Natalie; he will wait until she gives birth to tell her about Joyce. She will not understand, of course. For, really, there is nothing he can say to make their world right again. And she will recognize this, spitefully, and move the child away from Harper, away from troubled Kansas—to Pittsburgh or Berkeley or somewhere south.

Or maybe she will be able to forgive. And their relationship will gain a mysterious strength, heal over tightly like the lightning-shaped fracture along a bone. They will hold each other in bed at night, soft bodies fitted together, and never talk about Joyce Ives again. But always the indiscretion will remain this unspeakable part of their marriage, ugly as a birthmark, immune to surgery or even amputation. Reach for it with a blade and lose all.

"We need to leave," I say.

"But . . . I . . ."

There is nothing else. Not now. By the time Harper figures out what he is trying to say, Calvin and I are in the parking lot, backing out, with Harper in the doorway and Calvin making handprints against the frosted window on his side of the car.

This afternoon Kate has taken Calvin to Lawrence to shop for clothing, just a few new outfits, she says. Sitting on the top row of bleachers, I watch the basketball team scrimmage against itself. Noah walks along the far baseline, out of bounds, dripping wet from rain. He sinks Indian-style against the wall and starts his homework.

The demise of every man begins with a single pellet

of rain, my father once said, standing beside a basketball-team bus that had slid into a mud-filled ditch during a rainstorm in central Ohio. And so, too, did his own tragic undoing begin with an early-spring thunderstorm some years later.

At the time, I was still in high school and remember lying in the darkness, long after midnight, listening to the thunder and watching the flashes turn my room white. I must have drifted off, briefly, but when I awoke I heard my father in the kitchen speaking to my mother in a loud, distraught tone that made him sound like an outboard motor against the oak floorboards beneath my bed. Later, she came upstairs and called me to her bedroom. My father left the house again, in the rain, and she told me there had been an accident. It seemed Cooper Turo, who then was serving as an assistant coach, had been sent out to buy some beer. All the basketball coaches were working late, studying film in the offices at school. This was hardly uncommon the night before a game. Turo had gone to a convenience store not far from campus and, when he got to the cash register, found himself caught in the middle of a holdup.

At the trial some ten months later, the store owner testified that Turo had listened to everything the stickup man had told him to do. But as the man began to leave, Turo reached for his empty wallet on the floor and apparently his swaying reflection in the plate-glass window startled the man. There was only one blast, from a twelve-gauge shotgun that had been sawed down nine inches, and it removed the right side of Cooper Turo's head. And this was the hardest part: he lived for a full eight minutes after he was shot, coughing thick, syrupy oysters of blood that blocked his trachea, not only blood seeping from the inside but also the blood that was running down his face and into his mouth from his half-peeled skull. He couldn't breathe, the doctors told my father, and, in all likelihood, didn't even know it.

Turo had grown up in nearby Shaker Heights, which, like Lakeshire, is a suburb of Cleveland. The local press put a lot of pressure on my father to resign his post, speculating that it was at his insistence Turo went to purchase the beer; Turo should never have been at the convenience store in the first place. But the school stood by my father, and he remained Eastern Ohio University's head basketball coach for seven more years, until one cloudless July afternoon when my mother found him dead in our basement of heart failure. She told me several days afterwards, when I had returned home with Kate, that she just sat down there staring at him for the longest time. It was almost quiet, she said, except for the click, click, click of a spooled game film tapping against the warm projector.

When practice is finished, I sit in the basketball office waiting for Calvin and Kate to return from Lawrence. Hanging on the wall, there is a framed black-and-white photograph of Coach Miller's 1966 state championship team. The thing that strikes me most about this picture, other than the crew cuts, is how skinny and bone-straight everyone's legs seem to be. From afar, if you squint, they look like bars on a window.

At seven I leave, convinced I have made a mistake

and am supposed to meet them back at the house. The lights are off and Kate's white rental car is not in the driveway. Inside, the house is empty, and I turn up the heat and bring in the mail. Because it's late, I figure Calvin has already had his dinner, so I fix myself a peanut-butter sandwich and a glass of Scotch. There is not much mail: bills from the gas and telephone companies, an alumni magazine from Michigan Law School, a Stop 'n' Shop coupon flyer. On the bottom is a cream-colored envelope devoid of any postmarking, only my first name written across its middle in familiar black pen. Embossed in the upper left-hand corner is the red logo of Amis Motor Lodge. Nothing can feel like this, I think, leaning away from the table to catch my breath. I rip open the envelope from the side, also tearing the top edge from a matching sheet of Amis Motor Lodge stationery.

My eyes cannot read fast enough, but my brain understands, gleaning only those facts it needs to know. Kate has taken Calvin. They have gone away—to Texas, to Bali, to Budapest, she does not say. First, I am nauseous, laying my head on the table for support as my heart tries to shake its way up past my lungs. When I stand, my head fills with blood, quickly, and a shower of black spikes blurs my vision. The countertop is smooth and stable and I spread my hands flat, thumbs nearly touching. My arms have turned cold, pimpled with gooseflesh.

The woman at Amis Motor Lodge lets the phone ring eight times, I count, and when she finally answers, her voice is sharp and lucid and without compassion. She tells me Kate checked out this morning, and nothing else. She says it is not her policy to interrogate guests, so she doesn't know where Kate was headed. Before I can ask her anything else, she hangs up.

There are others to call—Kate's parents, the police—but I don't. The jukebox is playing loud and scratchy and Zoe tells me to wait while she switches to the phone in the kitchen. By the time she comes on again I am crouched down beside the stove, the telephone cord stretched nearly straight.

"Sorry, I couldn't hear you," she says.

In the background, someone asks for mashed potatoes and then there is the glassy sound of dishes being stacked.

"Calvin's gone," I say, clearly.

"What do you mean, he's gone?"

"He's *gone*! Kate's got him."

Now my voice is not so strong and it begins cracking, near the edges.

"Take it easy," says Zoe. "Yesterday Kate told me something about buying Calvin some clothes, in Lawrence."

"They're not in Lawrence." My tongue is bloated, heavy, and I run it along the scaly roof of my mouth. "She has taken him someplace else. Someplace I don't know."

"Listen, maybe they just—"

"There's a note."

For a moment Zoe is silent and I can hear the scurried clicking of a ballpoint pen.

"Stay where you are, Gordon. I'm coming over and we'll go look for them."

"She checked out of the motel," I say. "I know 'cause I called over there. Don't you think that's the first thing I'd do? Call over there?"

I feel queasy, sliding down the cabinet and allowing my head to rest on the cool floor.

"Gordon, what was that? Are you all right?"

I do not answer.

"Just wait for me, okay?"

I release the phone and watch it slingshot across the room, smacking into the far wall and slowly, methodically, bouncing on its cord until it rocks to an easy dangle.

In the frigid night air, Kate's note has turned soggy and limp beneath my fingers. The note is spread against my right thigh and every so often I examine it, reading the words again just to make sure, to make sure that this is all real. I'm sitting on the sill outside Calvin's window, his beaded Indian belt twisted into an empty knot. Below, the crooked river of wheat, dusted white, casts lean shadows in the wedge of floodlight.

All I want, now, at this moment, is my son. There are no tears, I cannot even cry.

I suck deep icy breaths that cause the sides of my tongue to curl. A steady stream of snot oozes from both nostrils, collecting on my upper lip.

"Calvin," I say, out loud.

Kate will not allow harm to come to him, she won't be careless. He is safe, my son, traveling the slick interstates seated in a rental car beside his mother, a woman he hardly knows. They will stop at a roadside convenience store, perhaps in Oklahoma or even as far north as Iowa, and she will buy him Moon Pies and wax lips and orange soda.

The panic is debilitating. My mind skips from thought to thought, rapidly, never settling with any certainty, any clarity, on a method for rescuing him. A numbness climbs from my calves as they rub against the gutter, feet dangling below—like Calvin's atop the kitchen counter or a restaurant booth. "They don't reach," he would say, because nothing fits his little body. Everything is too big. And now everything feels too large even for me, most especially this house. The only sound is a soft thumping as the insteps of my boots knock against each other.

This I remember, as my hand squeezes Kate's note into a tight, prickly ball. In Calvin's second week of life, days after we brought him home from the hospital and set up his basinet beside our bed, Kate decided to meet a friend for coffee, to take her initial rest from maternity. It was the first time in nine months, the first time ever, she and Calvin had been apart. Before she returned, Calvin began crying hysterically and although I tried to comfort him, singing while I carried him from room to room, he would not stop. Then, finally, I leaned in close so that our warm faces touched, and I offered my tongue. I don't know why I thought to do this, but he pulled my tongue into his mouth with force—sucking a lone, milkless nipple, tugging harder than I thought his tiny lips would allow.

Soon he was quiet and I placed him back on his blanket to sleep. I never did this, with my tongue, again and, in fact, never told Kate or anyone else about it. But at that moment, shortly after he had closed his eyes and turned silent, I knew this experience would provide me with a strange confidence. The confidence of fatherhood. No matter what, I would learn to adapt and find a way to make my son's life easier.

Except for now. There is nothing I can do but wait to make things whole.

The snow comes in flakes so pinhead-small I squint to see them blowing down near the light. Zoe pulls her truck around back, leaving the engine idling and door ajar as she runs to the house. Just before she reaches the porch she stops, looking up at the soles of my boots.

"Are you okay?" she says.

I shake my head. She grabs for my feet, but when her fingers peak they are still too far away.

"You want to come down?"

When I don't answer, she enters the house and I can hear her walking through the kitchen and up the staircase behind me.

"Nothing can make this better," I say, more to myself than to Zoe, who is now kneading my shoulders through the open window.

"It will be better when Calvin is back home."

"No. Nothing will ever feel the same for him. You lose something, some part of yourself . . . Maybe he won't trust people anymore. Maybe he won't trust *me*."

"He's too young. He won't understand."

"He'll understand."

When I was six my mother took me away. She awakened me at five-thirty in the morning and we loaded into her station wagon and drove the two and a half hours to her sister's place in Jamestown, New York. We didn't stop until we were only a mile or so from my aunt's and it was then, parked on a soot-sprayed curb beside the road, that my mother said we were leaving my father. We only stayed for three days and my mother never told me why we had left Ohio, but at the time I remember believing my father must have done something terribly wrong. Late, during our first night at my aunt's house, I lay nearly asleep on the living-room couch. I am kidnapped, I kept thinking, pulling a stuffed, knitted rabbit close to my throat. And this I understood: I would never feel exactly the same about either of my parents again.

Calvin, too, will understand. He won't forget what's happening to him, no matter what I say afterwards. No matter how soon he is found.

Zoe checks with Mrs. Grafton and then calls the rental-car company from next door to see if Kate has returned her Ford and taken Calvin somewhere by plane.

"She's still got the car," says Zoe, standing against the back wall, away from the cold air.

The evening passes and I make Zoe drive me along the back roads and smaller highways in search of my son. She does not need to tell me he is far away now, in another state. Still, I peer longingly into the windshield, my heart racing each time we spot a white vehicle—a car or a truck or, once, even a pale tractor. As the sun begins to pitch its way over the horizon, she parks at the base of my driveway and takes my hand, rubbing it against the stretched, oily skin of her forehead.

"We'll get him back," she says softly.

She holds me as the tears come, my head propped on her shoulder for support. We stay this way until finally, after nearly twenty minutes, she pushes me back and wipes my red, puckered eyes with the sleeve of her coat.

"Some tea will make you feel better."

But, of course, she is wrong.

The kitchen is exactly as I left it, with the telephone receiver still hanging loose and the Amis Motor Lodge envelope lying in pieces on the table. Near the sink, Zoe squeezes honey into two mugs of tea and then sits beside me.

"Can I fix you a sandwich?" she asks, steam rising to meet her face.

When I shake my head Zoe raises her arm, as if she is taking a vow, but she's only reaching to hang up the phone. Then she lights a cigarette and hands it to me. I take a long, slippery drag and let the smoke stay in my lungs for as long as I'm able—longer. After exhaling, I feel lightheaded and for the second time in a day lie flat, back-down, on the kitchen floor.

"Soon he will not remember me," I say. "She will hide him away and he will live a life separate from mine, a life where he can ride horses—his horses—whenever he wants."

"You're talking nonsense."

"She has money and can fight this in court. Really, I want to believe she couldn't win a custody battle. But there are things, things she could say that . . ."

"There is nothing," says Zoe. "You're a good father, Gordon. She *left* both of you."

In the quiet I can hear Mrs. Grafton slam the back door to her house, maybe after taking out the trash or sprinkling her stairs with rock salt.

"You don't know this," I say, sitting up with my back against one of the table legs. "But not long after Calvin was born, something happened." I take a breath. "There was a woman, a girl. She was sixteen and she lived with her family in the building beside our apartment. From the hallway, on the south side of our place, you could look directly into this girl's bedroom. At night, I used to leave Kate reading or watching TV in bed and take Calvin into the hall. There, I would stand with Calvin pressed to my chest watching this girl undress.

"One night, while I was staring out the window, I became pretty aroused." I stop, biting on my lower lip before continuing. "I was standing there holding Calvin with one arm while . . . well, fondling myself with the other. Kate had come up behind and it wasn't until she was nearly beside me that I heard her. She told me she knew I'd been watching the girl most nights. We had a big fight and she said I should get help, professional help. Like it was a problem.

"We didn't talk about it after that. Ever. It should be nothing, really. But you never know what people will use against you."

"There's no law against masturbation."

"Who knows what a judge is going to think of as deviant behavior. Especially for a parent."

"It will all be fine," says Zoe.

She pinches off the words so they sound tight, without conviction.

A stiffness has settled into my lower back when I awaken on the couch in the late morning. The few hours of sleep came in fitful bursts, leaving my shirt clinging to patches of sweat below my armpits and across the well of my chest. There is a sound, like the backfiring of a car, coming from outside, except this banging is consistent, breaking the silence again every minute or so.

Beyond our dirt basketball court, calf-deep in aged wheat, Zoe stands aiming a shotgun at a ragged sack of sand. The ground near her feet is speckled with empty, red shotgun casings once heavy with birdseed-sized pellets. She gives the gun a pump and then shoots, this time causing the frayed upper edge of the sack to rupture and spill in a runlet across its folded paunch.

"It helps clear my head," she says, watching as I move to her side. "The noise, the violence."

"That's comforting."

"I didn't mean for it to be comforting," says Zoe. "It's just something I do."

The sky is the flat, lifeless color of bone. Someone is burning cedar and the smell, like holiday spice, carries past us. Walking toward the house, Zoe puts her arm around my waist, bracing the gun against the raised leather seam of my belt. I can feel the warm barrel near my hip.

"Do you want to go out and look some more?" she asks.

"Where?" I say. "They could be fuckin' any place

by now. I want to look, I want to do something, *anything*, I just don't know what. Which direction would we even go in?"

She shrugs and leans the shotgun against the porch, butt-down. Then we sit quietly for a time, me on the ledge beside the fireplace and Zoe on the ottoman. When she rises, it is so she can make some calls from the telephone in the kitchen. The walls are thin and I can hear her speaking, first to the police and then to the school, letting them know I will not be at basketball practice today.

She brings me a glass of orange juice and I drink it in large, uneven swallows that sting my throat. After I finish, she takes the glass to the sink and rinses it of pulp. So now I'm truly helpless.

Yesterday, while I was waiting for her to come over, before I climbed onto the roof, I had this awful thought. It wasn't so much a thought as a wave of feeling that moved through me. *Relief.* Now that Calvin is gone, I'm free to do whatever I want. I have my life back. It belongs to me again.

She tilts her head, slightly, and dries her hands in the fabric of her shirt.

But almost instantly the sensation passed and once more I was worried. Because I don't need to feel relief if it means not having Calvin. He is a part of the only life I want.

She takes my face in her hands, still clammy from dishwater, and kisses me on the swirling cowlick near the crest of my scalp.

After the police leave, it begins snowing again, this time in flakes so weighted with moisture they disappear on impact. The photograph I gave the officer for identification purposes is one of Calvin sitting on the hood of my car, wearing an orange T-shirt and khaki shorts. He is holding a book of Africa my mother sent him and the pages are winged open across his lap, revealing an upside-down color plate of a giraffe grazing on the thorny tufts of an acacia tree. It would be a fine photograph, except Calvin's eyes are gazing to his left, locked on something beyond the snapshot's borders. The picture was taken last summer and I cannot, for the life of me, remember what he was staring at.

The telephone rings while I'm in the bathroom and when Zoe yells for me, immediately, her voice brittle, I know that the call concerns Calvin. Standing beside the coffee table, Zoe looks pained and she thrusts the receiver toward me.

"It's Kate," says Zoe, in a gritty whisper.

I can feel the hairs along the back of my neck tremble skyward.

"Kate," I say, sucking in quick mouthfuls of air, "just tell me he's all right. Tell me he's fine."

"Sure. He's okay,"she says, pausing before her next sentence. "He's watching TV and playing with a tow truck I bought him at this gas station near Carlton."

"Where are you?"

"It's blue."

"What?"

"It's blue. The tow truck, it's blue. It was only four

dollars with a fill-up. That's something I know, now. Little boys like toy trucks. Tow trucks, dump trucks, eighteen-wheelers, snowplows, whatever."

"Kate," I say, holding my still-unfastened belt as I sit down. "Where are you?"

She tells me they are at a motel in Jefferson City, Missouri. She even gives me directions and says her car is parked out front.

"It shouldn't take you more than four hours," she says. "If you go the speed limit."

Before we hang up, I'm quiet for a moment, thinking that four hours is a long time and Kate could change her mind. Also, I want to talk to Calvin, to hear in his own lonely voice that he is fine, and, indeed, Kate does not know what she's talking about: all boys do not like toy trucks. Calvin, for one, would rather have had some brightly colored markers or an oversized plastic ring he could move from one finger to the next. But it's unlikely they carry items such as these at gas stations in middle Missouri.

When I inhale like I'm preparing to say something else, if only to keep alive the connection, Kate says, "We'll be here," and then there is honest silence followed by the hum of a dial tone.

Zoe and I stop only once, near the Missouri border, to fill her truck with gasoline. She smokes a cigarette away from the pump, down where the asphalt changes to long, brown grass. A man driving an Airstream camper takes his dog for a walk beside a hurricane fence pushed crooked by wind. Later, when we are driving again, Zoe asks me if I thought the man was alone in his camper. Alone, of course, except for his dog.

"I don't know," I say, concentrating on the road.

"You'd think if his family was in there they'd want to come out for some air. Or maybe to stretch their legs."

This is the last thing either of us says for nearly three hours, until we reach Jefferson City. It is dark and the snow has turned to rain, falling in black, greasy sheets. The wipers squeak as they rake against the windshield. Our highway exit is not well lighted and we don't see it until we're already half past. Then we drive six or so miles farther, until the first open passage back across the median strip.

"We'll have to remember to read the directions off the highway in reverse," says Zoe.

The motel is a Super 8 at the western edge of town. Zoe spots it first, from the right side of the truck. As we pull into the parking lot, yellow and red lights from a rotating neon sign blink through our windows, laying fuzzy shadows across Zoe's face. Now we are moving slowly, waiting for Kate's rental car to rise in the glass of my door. My heart runs with a fury and I can feel the new blood, especially as it sinks past my temples in tingling waves. Kate's car finally appears at the twisting S-curve of the motel from behind a dark green van.

"Look," says Zoe, sliding her hand across the dashboard.

Glowing saffron in the dappled motel light, Calvin stands beneath the concrete awning with his right arm extended. More than anything I want to lift him, hold him so tight that our chests lock, swelling to the same stilted rhythm. But I won't, I decide. Nothing that will alarm him. As I approach, I notice he is holding a small plastic measuring scoop in his right hand, the kind that comes free with a tin of coffee. At first, I'm not sure what words to say. And then I settle simply for asking him what he is doing.

"I'm seein' how much water will fill this," he says.

As I run my hand down his back, he dips his shoulder as if to shake me loose. Then, when I move behind him, nearer to the doorway of Kate's room, he asks if we are going home in a voice so genuine, so unfettered by troubles, that I can only smile. Perhaps Zoe was right and soon, very soon, everything will be fine.

"Yes," I say. "In a few minutes."

"Good."

The lapse in concentration that occurs when he speaks causes his arm to stir, spilling some of the collected rainwater on the already wet cement. I bend down beside him, tilting my head so it is almost touching his face.

"Pal?" I start, in a broken falsetto. "Can you do something for me? Can you give me a kiss?"

Keeping his eyes focused ahead, he turns and gives me a peck on the cheek. Again, he loses some of his water, and this time he lets out a loud "Sheesh." I point to Zoe, who is still sitting in the truck with her legs hanging out of the open door.

"Will you keep an eye on him?" I ask.

The only light in Kate's motel room comes from a shaded desk lamp positioned between the twin beds. Several of Calvin's toys lie scattered across the floor, including his new blue tow truck. This feeling will not escape me: the same heightened sensation of being in a basketball game with only seconds remaining and my team ahead by a point. As the other team tries to inbound the ball, I'm guarding the baseline, sprinting laterally from end to end, my arms waving wildly in an attempt to deflect the pass. Things move at an exaggeratedly slow pace and if this were real I would notice what I might normally gloss over, like a solitary bead of sweat tumbling down the referee's forehead, or the drawstring on a player's shorts as it flicks like a tongue at his waist. Soon, once the ball has been tossed into play, things will move quickly again and then it will be over. But for now, in this very immediate moment, I am capable of anything.

The motel room is warm and I can hear the accordion-style radiator against the far wall clanking with fresh coursing steam. At my side, the window has turned foggy and I look to see if Calvin has drawn any of his familiar etchings, but there is nothing. A pungent smell like kerosene or hairspray sifts through the air. My knee brushes against the near bed and when I look down, past the comforter stretched close as animal hide, I can see a page from Calvin's coloring book, the one of the baker, resting, slightly folded, beside the headboard. On the other bed, Kate's suitcase lies open with its guts stacked in neat, random piles. There are also several sets of new clothing belonging to Calvin: stiff indigo jeans, furry sweatshirts of green and gray, tube socks, and a pair of boots that are much too high for him to wear comfortably.

The night Kate first arrived in Tarent, I remember standing on the front lawn, gesturing back toward the house and declaring in a bold, confident tone that this was the way Calvin and I lived. Now, as my eyes scan the cluttered motel room, its walls pressing close, I can't help but think that this is the way Calvin and Kate would have lived. For a while, anyway. Until decisions were made. Decisions made by someone else.

A creaking comes from the bathroom as the door pushes open and Kate, dressed in a white terry-cloth robe, is at my side. Before I can think or, maybe, because I have had time to think, I swing out with my left arm, catching her flush with the back of my hand across her cheekbone. She drops to the floor, holding her face and tucking her thighs against her chest for protection.

Leaning down, I extend my hand and help her back on her feet. Once standing, she takes me by the elbow and walks to the edge of the bed.

"I deserved that," she says, touching the salmon-colored petal above her cheekbone.

There is a towel beside the bathroom sink and I soak it in cold water before wringing it damp and then handing it to her. She holds it gently against the side of her face, pulling it back every few seconds and folding it anew for a fresh, cooler swatch of cloth.

"I'm sorry about all this," she says, taking a seat on the end of the bed. Several times her voice crumbles, as if she's going to burst into tears, but she is able to swallow them down like wandering hiccups. When she crosses her legs the motion causes a stack of Calvin's new clothing, behind her, to fall on its side. "I just didn't expect . . ." She pauses, dabbing higher on her cheek. "I guess I don't know what I expected."

"I never hit a woman before," I say. "Not even when I was little."

She takes my hand and rubs it briefly, across the joints, before letting go again.

"There are so many things I don't know about him," she says. "Important things. Like sometimes he drinks his orange juice from Budweiser bottles, or when he has pancakes, he wants them rolled into log-shaped tubes that he can spear with a fork and eat like a hot dog on a stick."

"You learn over time."

"Time's the one thing I never had with him. I suppose that's what made me do this. However crazy it may sound, I thought I could force motherhood, on both of us." She picks a thread from her face and flicks it to the floor. "I knew it wouldn't last. I knew I couldn't have him forever. I just wanted him to spend some time with his mother. Alone. Like maybe we were going away on vacation, the two of us, and none of the stuff between you and me had ever happened. I wanted to pretend that I knew things about him—like the beer bottles and pancakes."

"This didn't exactly work out like we planned," I say, sitting down beside her. "The visit, I mean. Maybe I shouldn't have been so difficult. I don't know," I start, straightening my feet so they both point toward the bathroom. "For a long time I thought you should pay for your actions."

"And now?"

"Now I don't know what to think."

She nods.

"You know what it was?" asks Kate. "You know what made me finally call you? He had a stomachache. I think it was something he ate for lunch, maybe the maple syrup or the home fries." She is trembling, so, for support, she knots her fingers together and lays them across her belly. "Anyway, we had just gotten back to the room when he started complaining. For a while, I was really scared. He was rolling on the floor, kicking and screaming. I didn't know what to do. I tried massaging his stomach and putting a hot compress on it and I even went to the drugstore to get him some Pepto. But he wouldn't take it. He just wailed. Then, finally, I locked myself in the bathroom and started crying myself. Quite a picture: me in there and Calvin out here, both bawling our eyes out. Some mother, I thought. That's when I called you.

"By the time I got off the phone, he was fine. He was playing with his toys and watching TV. But when it mattered most, I couldn't make him better."

"That's how it is sometimes," I say.

She shrugs, and then says, "I love him so dearly. But maybe I was right, maybe this is not the time for me to be a mother. At least not every day."

Parenting is rarely convenient, I'm tempted to say.

"When I was in the bathroom, alone, all I wanted was for him to shut up, to shut his mouth and . . . and go away. I don't have the patience. But you know what I remembered? I started thinking about the time we went to visit my folks in Texas, not long after Calvin was born.

It was hot and muggy and we went to the beach. Near the end of the day, when we were waiting for my parents to pick us up, it began to rain. I remember you took the lid off our drinks cooler and placed Calvin inside. Then you covered it, lightly, with a blanket. This isn't the first time that incident has crossed my mind. Sometimes I'll think of him as being like that when he's with you. Of being safe, in a cool, dry place."

She lets the towel fall to her lap. Then she leans close and kisses me above my eyebrow.

"Do you think I could come visit from time to time?" she asks.

"Maybe," I say, if only to fill the silence.

"I told him I'd take him riding over the summer. And next fall I want to watch him leave for his first day of school. That would be nice."

She brings her knees together, allowing the flesh at the base of her thighs to squeeze against itself.

"I'd like to say goodbye to him," she says. "If that's okay."

When I open the door, Calvin is no longer collecting raindrops. He is sitting near Zoe inside the cab of her truck and I can see them both looking at pictures in a magazine. He comes to my side when I call him.

"Your mother is leaving," I say.

"When are *we* leavin'?"

"Soon. But she wants to say goodbye. You won't see her for a little while."

He flashes a quizzical look. "We're going riding."

"Later," I say. "In the spring or summer, when it gets warm."

The motel room seems darker now and the sober twang of slide guitar rises from a radio on the nightstand. Kate holds open her arms and beckons Calvin in a voice as fragile as a reed. He walks over and touches her, tenderly, on the damaged line of her cheek.

"Hold me," she says, grabbing him beneath his spiky shoulder blades.

She rocks him from side to side in time to the music. Then she raises his shirt and places her face flush against the skin of his chest.

"Will you dance with me?" she asks.

Calvin does not know how to dance, except for a lame, spastic rendition of the jitterbug that I taught him about a year ago. He looks to me for help.

"He doesn't really know how," I say.

"Nonsense," says Kate. "It's easy."

She lifts Calvin onto a chair so his head nearly reaches her collarbone. Together they move to Kate's music, Calvin kicking his feet awkwardly to a rhythm of his own.

"No, honey," says Kate into his ear. "Slower."

When Calvin still doesn't get it, she just holds him, tight this time.

"Slower," she says, again, almost to herself. "Dance real slow."

She wants to make these final, fleeting moments of motherhood last. Soon, Calvin has had enough and he pulls away.

"Okay," she says, kissing him on the mouth and nose before letting go. "That's all."

Then she gathers his belongings and places them

into a satchel. She kisses him, again, and escorts us to the door. "Next time I see you, we'll go riding," she says.

Calvin nods.

"Good."

And that's the last thing Kate says before closing the door behind Calvin and me.

"She doesn't have ice cream," whispers Calvin, randomly, as he tugs at the hem of my jacket.

In the shining headlights of Zoe's truck, the concrete walk has turned as white as the powdery undersides of scrub-oak leaves. Before Calvin climbs onto the seat, beside Zoe, he bends down and makes a funny face at the truck's silvery grillwork. There is no one close enough to see this except me.

ABOUT THE AUTHOR

Michael Grant Jaffe received an M.F.A. from Columbia University and is a special contributor to *Sports Illustrated*. He was born in Cleveland and lives in New York City.